Death Dances at Yuma

Turned into a saloon bum by tragedy, Josie Dooley has the opportunity to redeem himself. The love of a good woman and the promise of high financial reward has him accepting a gunrunning mission down the hazardous Gila Trail.

Fighting Apaches along the trail, Dooley is under threat from a vengeance-bound gunfighter, and is betrayed by the man who hired him. When the beautiful and mysterious Juanita appears out of the wilderness, she has Dooley's emotions in turmoil. Now Dooley is forced by happenstance into being the only one who can save the territory's population from massacre by the Apache chief Galvez Chama.

It is a daunting task for a man only recently recovered from alcoholism, but, with Juanita at his side, Dooley must take on a fight that already appears to have been lost.

By the same author

The Forgotten Man
The Protector
Danger in the Desert
The Hunting Man
The Long Journey
He Rode With Quantrill
Missouri Blood Trail
Breakout at Salem Gaol
Canyon of Crooked Shadows
San Carlos Horse Soldier
Midnight Lynching
Logan's Legacy
Railroad Rangers

Death Dances at Yuma

TERRY MURPHY

A Black Horse Western

ROBERT HALE · LONDON

© Terry Murphy 2003
First published in Great Britain 2003

ISBN 0 7090 7231 7

Robert Hale Limited
Clerkenwell House
Clerkenwell Green
London EC1R 0HT

The right of Terry Murphy
to be identified as author of this work has been
asserted by her in accordance with the Copyright,
Design and Patents Act 1988.

Typeset by
Derek Doyle & Associates, Liverpool.
Printed and bound in Great Britain by
Antony Rowe Limited, Wiltshire.

One

It was late afternoon, the quiet time of day in the Nevada House saloon. An undersized bartender stretched up on his toes lighting oil lamps. A drunk was draped over the bar, either asleep or in an alcoholic stupor. A gambler sat at a table, his deceptively mild-face contradicted by his hard, watchful eyes. Manipulating a pack of cards, he exercised his long, flexible fingers in readiness for the hours to come. Framed in an office doorway at the rear of the bar room, was Dolores Morelos, the owner of the saloon. The shadows were kind to her, hiding the lines about the mouth and too much rouge upon the cheek. Her dress was rich, the diamonds glittering in the new light from the smoking oil lamps. There was an air of detachment about her.

Yet she and the other two sober occupants of

the room came alert when a stranger pushed open the swinging doors. The bartender moved surreptitiously closer to the scattergun kept under the bar. Though the gambler didn't noticeably shift position, the holstered .45 at his right hip had come within easy reach. Dolores Morelos moved forward a few steps.

All three were made wary by the unusually early hour of the newcomer's entrance. The saloon's patrons normally arrived out of the dark of night rather than twilight. It meant that the stranger was there for a purpose, which could spell trouble for one or all of them. Dangerous men often drifted in from the tall-grass valleys and high mesas in the lofty range of snow-capped peaks and rugged mountains that surrounded the town of Mesquite.

The stranger turned his head first to the left and then to the right to send a calculating glance travelling round the big room. He was a stocky, muscular man, past middle age and standing five and one-half feet in height. The rugged features of his face reflected a callous disposition. His dress was that of a gentleman, polished tan boots, pencil-striped trousers, a pearl-grey vest with white pearl buttons, and a long, pale-grey coat. The tan-coloured cravat he wore matched the soft Stetson that he carried in one hand. Worn short, his hair was brown with a white dusting around the edges. He was unarmed as far as the customary wearing of a gunbelt was concerned, but a bulge in the left armpit of his coat suggested that a small gun was holstered there.

He strode forward, ordering, 'Whiskey' from the left side of his mouth as he passed the bartender and walked on to come to a halt beside the collapsed drunk. Reaching to pick up an empty bottle, the newcomer pushed the neck of it under the drunk's chin to lever his head up off the counter.

Pressure from the bottle forcing his head back at an awkward angle, the drunk peered blearily at the stranger through bloodshot eyes. Despite his unhealthy pallor, he was a young man, somewhere around the age of thirty-five. Then his eyes glazed over before closing. His chin slid off the neck of the bottle and his head dropped to hit the wooden bar with a thud.

Using the bottle roughly, the newcomer prised up the drunk's head again. This time the red eyes opened and stayed open as he glared angrily at his tormentor.

'Are you Dooley, Josie Dooley?' the man holding the bottle asked.

When no answer came from the drunk, Dolores Morelos called from where she leaned against the doorjamb of her office, 'He's Josie Dooley. What do you want with him, mister?'

'That's my business.' The hard man glared at her. High cheekbones gave his eyes an Oriental slant. They were wintry grey eyes that were as bleak as death.

'This being my place means it ain't just your business,' Dolores argued calmly.

'Stay out of this, ma'am,' the newcomer advised, as he dug the neck of the bottle hard into Dooley's throat.

The man shuffling the deck of cards looked up as if considering going to the drunk's rescue. But he cancelled the notion and concentrated on the fan of playing cards he had spread on the table in front of him.

Pain seemed to force the alcohol fumes from the drunk's mind, and he asked in a strangled voice, 'Who are you?'

'Kane Prowler,' the newcomer announced.

'The name means nothing to me, Prowler,' Dooley said, slurring his words. He added. 'And I'd sure recommend that you take that bottle out of my neck.'

'I know the reputation you once had, Dooley, but right now you don't seem to be in no fit state to go threatening folk.' Prowler's hard face split apart in a white-toothed grin.

'Maybe, maybe not,' Dooley said with an indifferent shrug, before suddenly and surprisingly springing into action.

Left arm knocking aside the hand in which Prowler held the bottle, Dooley swung a right-hand punch at Prowler's head. But drink had slowed his reflexes and destroyed his co-ordination. With a smile fixed on his hard face, Prowler swayed his upper body so that the punch went past his head harmlessly. Then he countered viciously. Kicking the drunken Dooley's feet out from underneath him, at the same time he reversed the bottle in his hand so that he was holding the neck. Quick as a flash as Dooley was falling, Prowler cracked him hard across the skull with the bottle.

Crashing down on to the brass foot rail, Dooley's unconscious body did a half roll on the sawdust-covered plank floor and lay still, face down. Turning away from him, Prowler picked up the glass of rye the bartender had slid toward him. Downing the whiskey in one swallow, he then tossed a coin on the bar as Dolores Morelos walked up slowly.

Smoothing her dress, she looked down with a sigh to where Dooley lay like a bundle of dirty rags. Little wrinkles of perplexity creased her brow. Dolores raised her eyes to Prowler. She stood straight and slender, facing the stranger with level gaze. 'Folk about here don't take kindly to this sort of thing, mister.'

'Folk where I come from keep out of other folk's affairs, ma'am,' Prowler politely but pointedly retorted.

'There ain't no glory in beating up on a drunk, mister. Josie Dooley ain't no more than a saddle tramp nowadays.'

'No, you got it wrong, ma'am,' the hard man disagreed. The unconscious Dooley, face down in the sawdust, was making a snorting, choking sound, and Prowler used the toe of a boot to move his head to one side. The noise ceased. Sawdust speckled the curls on Dooley's black-haired head. Prowler went on talking to Dolores. 'A saddle bum's got both a horse and a saddle. I reckon as how Dooley sold those two things long ago.'

'That is no reason to come striding in here to pick on him, mister.'

Prowler corrected her. 'He picked on me. I came here to make him an offer, give him the chance to rejoin the human race.'

'I'd say that's the last thing Josie wants,' Dolores said, sadly.

'You kind of close to him, ma'am?' an interested Prowler enquired, studying her. There was a fineness to her features that was now no more than a memory that hinted at descent from an old New England family.

'Nobody's close to Dooley,' Dolores replied. 'On his better days he helps out here in the Nevada House, cleaning up and suchlike. I let him sleep in a shed out back.'

She signalled to the bartender, who slid a bottle of rye toward her. Dolores refilled Prowler's glass. Thanking her, Prowler raised his glass in a silent and unspecified toast before taking a drink. 'Don't go condemning me, ma'am. I don't see Dooley as a busted flush. I grant you that a gunslinger that takes to drink because he's lost his nerve ain't worth a light, but that ain't the case with Dooley. A man who loses his woman is a heap different. An *hombre* living a precarious life finds a good woman is necessary to satisfy the emotional side of his nature. What happened to Josie Dooley was a real tragedy, ma'am.'

Dolores bit her bottom lip, leaving the indent of her teeth as she whispered regretfully, 'I know nothing of his personal life. What exactly are you offering him?'

'If he joins up with me he'll either become a very rich man or a very dead man,' Prowler answered.

'Josie Dooley would probably prefer the second choice, mister,' Dolores said solemnly.

'Then it's likely that I won't disappoint him, ma'am,' Prowler assured her, as he watched Dooley stir into life.

From the street outside came a rumbling of many hooves and the lowing of cattle as a herd was driven to the stockyard at the bottom of town. When the herd had gone there was total silence. Strangely, the entire atmosphere in the saloon had changed. Everything was still until the gambler broke the silence with the fluttering rattle of pasteboards as he flicked a pack of cards from one hand to the other. This familiar sound brought the bar room back to normality.

Raising his backside high, Dooley kept his chest on the floor to allow the blood to flow to his head. Then slowly he made it up on to his feet. Swaying, he gradually got his bearings and turned to face Prowler, who took the precaution of placing his hand on the bar close to the bottle that he had used as a club.

Seeing this, Dooley raised both hands in a gesture of surrender. He spoke weakly. 'One day you'll pay for downing me with that bottle, Prowler, but right now I'm not looking for trouble.'

'What are you looking for, Dooley?' Prowler enquired.

'Nothing.'

'Everybody's looking for something.'

With a negative shake of his head, Dooley said mournfully, 'Looking's fine, Prowler; it's when you do the finding that everything goes ass-backwards.'

'What I've got to say will have you thinking different,' Prowler told him.

With a swishing of skirts, Dolores went behind the bar to fill a glass and pass it to Dooley. He drank slowly as if performing some kind of a ritual. Unconsciousness had sobered him. The reviving effect of this one drink was visible. Eyes clearing to become an almost startling blue, he looked at Prowler.

'I'm listening,' Dooley said.

Prowler explained. 'I'm a businessman, Dooley.'

'A businessman who packs a derringer in a shoulder holster,' Dooley observed drily.

'Nice to see that you ain't completely lost your touch, Dooley,' Prowler grinned. 'I'm here because I need a good man for a tough job.'

'And I was recommended,' Dooley snorted cynically. Stretching out his right arm, he studied the tremor in his hand. 'Take a look at that, Prowler. I sure couldn't hit a bull's ass with a handful of banjos.'

'A couple of days drying out and you'll be as good as new,' Prowler predicted. 'You've had it rough, Dooley.'

Death Dances at Yuma

This reference to something personal displeased Dooley. Face stiff, expressionless, he said in a half-whisper, 'You talk too much, Prowler.'

'I came here to talk,' Prowler retorted. 'I'm offering you your self-respect back, Dooley, and a small fortune to go with it.'

Shaking his head, Dooley declined the offer, 'You're about ten years too late, Prowler. You want a young-blood if you're looking for a tie-down man.'

'No,' Prowler disagreed, signalling to Dolores to refill the glasses of Dooley and himself. 'I can get all the young hothead fast-draws I want, but the lot of them together ain't worth a plugged nickel. You're the only man for me, Dooley.'

Dooley's hand shook as he raised his glass, and Dolores reached across and put a hand on his arm. It had the look of a friendly gesture, but she had steadied Dooley's arm, saving him from embarrassment. She gave him a quick, fond, but almost, shy smile.

'I'm not agreeing to anything, but say your piece, Prowler,' Dooley said, looking to Dolores and the bartender for another drink, but Prowler took the empty glass from Dooley's hand and sent it sliding fast out of reach along the bar.

'If you're siding me, Dooley, that was your last

drink,' Prowler warned. 'There's big money waiting for us out there. I want a fighting man who is also a thinking man.'

Looking ill, sweat glistening on his forehead, Dooley placed an elbow on the bar to keep himself upright. He sounded breathless. 'The man you need, Prowler, is the Josie Dooley you heard tell about, not the Josie Dooley you're talking to right now.'

Prowler disagreed. 'They're one and the same person. The only one who can do what I've got in mind.'

'Which is?'

'I've two wagons loaded with rifles for delivery to Fort Yuma.'

'Along the Gila Trail, Prowler?'

Prowler gave a curt nod.

Dooley, really weak now, turned to face the bar, using both elbows to support himself. 'Then you can count me out! You'll need to go the long way around. Maybe pack horses or a head-and-tail string of mules will traverse the direct Gila Trail, but wheeled vehicles won't get through.'

'You know the trail, which is one of the reasons for me wanting you along,' Prowler said with a satisfied nod.

'What you want is a mountain man, Prowler. Someone like Tom Fitzpatrick, for instance. If you get lucky and make it, then you're not going to get rich on the pittance the government pays.'

'This ain't a government assignment, Dooley. The Apaches are acting in a real disagreeable manner down around the Colorado River, torturing and slaughtering the settlers wholesale. General Williams at the fort ain't getting the supplies he needs from the Government. He's organized the settlers into a volunteer army, but they need rifles and are ready to pay the earth for them so as to defend themselves. We get them two wagons there and we'll make ourselves a fortune.'

'Money we'd never live to spend,' Dooley pointed out. 'I'm not ready to die yet.'

'You're not exactly living now, Dooley,' Prowler remarked sarcastically.

'I'd prefer being half dead here than all dead down at Yuma,' Dooley said softly. 'You're asking a man who can't stand up unaided, who can't see straight, to walk out of that door ready to shoot straight! You're a man looking for a miracle, Prowler.'

'I'm a man who works miracles, Dooley,' Prowler replied confidently. 'I'm offering you what is probably your last chance in life. Show me that you can make the effort, and I'll back you all the way.'

'You can clean up in my place, Josie,' Dolores

offered. 'I've no right to tell you what to do, but I see this as a real opportunity for you.'

Putting a trembling hand on her shoulder, Dooley said, 'I know what you say is right, Dolores, and it's right kind of you. You'll get a share if we make it to Yuma and back.'

'I'm not looking for money. You just remember where I am and come back to me.'

Taking a roll of banknotes from his back pocket, Prowler peeled off six and laid them on the bar. 'Get yourself fixed up with a haircut, a shave, and a decent set of clothes. You spend one cent of that on redeye and you'll have me to reckon with. Do you hear me?'

'I hear you,' Dooley muttered.

'We'll pick up the Gila Trail at Santa Fe. You be outside here right after sun-up tomorrow, and be stone cold sober.'

Pushing himself upright, leaving just his left hand on the bar to support him, Dooley spoke shakily. 'I'll be there, Prowler.'

Two

'This is a sight easier than I anticipated,' Prowler remarked, as they moved the two heavily laden wagons along the Chihuahua Trade Road.

'Don't let this fool you, Prowler,' Dooley warned, his voice faint and weak.

He had the shakes, too. Up on an unsprung wagon seat he was suffering bouts of convulsions so bad that often he came close to dropping the reins.

The morning they had left Mesquite he had felt terribly ill. He had not touched a drop of alcohol, and had, with Dolores' help, smartened himself up to look the part. But it was all on the surface. Beneath the new clothes and despite a haircut and a clean shave, he was still a wreck.

His physical condition had deteriorated since Kane Prowler had been moderately supportive but outrightly unsympathetic. He had bought two Conestoga wagons so new that the smell of red and blue paint still clung to them. In a land where the average mule gave out on the first day, Prowler had the fmest team of mules that could be secured, and it was plain that he expected Dooley soon to come up to the same high standard.

'This is the easy bit, Prowler.' Dooley pointed to where mountains closed in on the east side of the Rio Grande river, and menacing hills walled the west side. 'When we cross the Rio Grande, to reach the Gila Trail we have to face the *Jornada del Muerte*.'

'My Spanish ain't so good Dooley,' Prowler complained.

'The Journey of Death,' Dooley translated.

'A desert?'

'That's right,' Dooley confirmed. 'Hotter than all get-out.'

Two days out of Santa Fe, and in barren country that would not feed a single jackrabbit, Dooley's prediction became a reality. The sun rose high, beating down with a relentless fierceness out of a tinny sky. With the going hard, they had not been making more than seven or eight miles a day. The heat was intolerable. Built for plains travel, the wagons were useless in the desert. They had iron-tyred wheels that,

Death Dances at Yuma

smaller in front than at the back, sank deep into the sand, and they lost a lot of time as the wagons bogged down.

Semi-conscious for most of the time during which they had fought their way across the desert, bathed in sweat and sometimes completely unconscious, Dooley somehow made it. He was immensely relieved to see that the mountains up ahead were near, looming yellow, grey, and brown. He could make out the rocky ridges and the shadowy canyons. The tiny dark blotches of a few hours ago were now recognizable as junipers and stunted pines.

They headed for the old Indian pass through the Black Range mountains. It was a rugged trail that took them through narrow canyons separated by towering rocky ridges, but the going was easier on the mules. They crossed the summit and were rewarded by a less difficult trail, good grazing, and cooler weather.

Even so, the better conditions did little to ease Dooley's distress. The thought of going on was daunting, but to go back would mean that he would perish in trying to cross the desert again.

Three bartenders were working flat-out in the Nevada House. Dolores Morelos covertly watched Ace Ormsbie, the house gambler. She moved along the bar to serve him as, with a game over, he walked up to order a drink. He was a slim man with wavy fair hair, pale-grey eyes and features that were almost too perfect. Dolores had heard big, rough men, duped by Ormsbie's looks, jeer that he was as 'purty as any gal'. Only the lucky few lived to regret making the remark. The gambler was fearless and fast on the draw.

'Help yourself, Ace,' Dolores invited, sliding an empty glass and a full bottle of whiskey across the bar to him.

They were friends, but not so close as they once had been. What could have been a significant relationship between her and the gambler had cooled from about the time Josie Dooley had staggered into Mesquite.

Ormsbie asked, 'What's the occasion, Dolores?'

'I'm just feeling generous, Ace.' Dolores smiled disarmingly. 'Do I need an excuse to give a friend a drink?'

'Not an excuse' – the vaguely amused gambler shook his head – 'but a reason. Nobody gets anything for nothing in this world, except perhaps a bullet in the head.'

'You are a cynic, Ace,' Dolores complained.

Pouring a drink, Ormsbie raised the glass. Looking over the rim at Dolores, he urged, 'Let's have it.'

'Have what?' she responded, with arch innocence.

'Tell me the favour you want from me, or ask the question you want answered.'

Dolores pulled a face. 'Isn't it boring to be so wise that you can predict just about everything, Ace?'

'It's what has enabled me to survive for forty years, Dolores, knowing what the *hombre* across the table is going to do before he knows it himself.'

'I'll get to the point,' Dolores said, rushing her words. 'You knew Josie Dooley way back, didn't you?'

With a negative shake of his head, the gambler replied, 'I knew of him, but I didn't know him until he came here, and by then he wasn't worth knowing.'

'Was he worth knowing in the old days, Ace?'

'I guess so,' Ormsbie shrugged. 'When he was marshal down in Tres Piños, he was the fastest gun I ever saw.'

'Faster than you?' Dolores, having seen Ormsbie involved in gunplay several times, asked incredulously.

'Luckily, I never found out.'

'Lucky, for whom?'

'Probably me,' the gambler admitted.

'That stranger said something about Dooley being involved in a tragedy.'

Death Dances at Yuma

Pouring himself another drink, the gambler became uneasy. 'It isn't a story fit for a woman to hear.'

'I'm tougher than most women, Ace.'

'I guess that's the truth, Dolores, and I've always admired you for it,' the gambler conceded. 'I wasn't involved, so I can only tell it second-hand like. As town marshal, Dooley shot dead a no-good Mexican by the name of Hernando Corsicana. Later on, Dooley married Holly Wadsworth, the daughter of a rancher. The two of them were out shopping together one afternoon. Holly went into a haberdashery, and Dooley waited outside for her. That was when Alonzo Corsicana, Hernando's half-brother, stepped up at the far end of the sidewalk. Hell-bent on vengeance, Alonzo drew on Dooley. Dooley slapped leather. Just as the two of them fired, so did Holly come out of the store all-unsuspecting.'

'Oh, God!' Dolores moaned, eyes closed as she imagined the scene.

'Holly took a slug that blew a mighty large hole in her chest, and died right there on the sidewalk.'

'Instead of avenging his brother, the Mexican killed Josie's wife?' Dolores gasped.

'Maybe so, maybe not,' Ormsbie replied. 'No one could be sure then or ever since, whether it was Alonzo Corsicana's bullet, or a slug from Josie

Dooley's gun that killed Holly.'

Dolores asked tremulously, 'What happened?'

'Alonzo left town, Dooley prepared to go after him, but decided to have a drink first. Trouble was that he couldn't stop drinking and he never did go after Corsicana.'

'What an awful thing to happen,' Dolores sighed. 'Josie has had to live with it.'

'You've kind of got Dooley on your mind an awful lot, Dolores,' the gambler observed.

'He's a good man, Ace, and I guess that I have feelings for him,' Dolores admitted.

Looking at her fondly, Ormsbie warned. 'Be careful not to get hurt, Dolores. When men sink as low as Josie Dooley has, there isn't usually any way back up.'

'I think that Josie has found a way,' Dolores said, hopefully.

The cry of an owl wakened Dooley from a fitful sleep. He listened for the answering call and would have rolled himself in his blankets again had he not known getting back to sleep would be an impossibility. Somewhere in the trees a night bird trilled mindlessly up and down the scale, then all went quiet again. The fragrance of burning green juniper from the long dead camp-fire was still on the air.

Death Dances at Yuma

The cold that he felt came from deep inside of him. It radiated from a skeleton that felt like ice, freezing his flesh and making his skin sore. Having hoped to have regained at least some of his strength along the trail, he felt despair and a rage of defeat. Sitting shivering with a blanket over his shoulders in the shadow of a thorn hedge, he accepted that he had to wait out the long hours of cheerless darkness until a dismal dawn.

The snarl of a coyote caused Prowler to stir in his bedroll. Muttering something unintelligible, he settled down to sleep again and Dooley remained alone in the night. He was filled with regret.

Once his life had been well regulated, with each day purposeful and the future assured. After four proud years as marshal of a town fifty times wilder than Mesquite, he had married Holly and they had planned for the future. He would spend one more year as town marshal, and then they were going to buy themselves a small spread. It had been a wonderful dream that hadn't come true, and never would.

Now everything was uncertain. Could he survive tomorrow without a drink? Was there any hope of Prowler and himself surviving on the perilous Gila Trail? If so, would Dolores Morelos be waiting for him? Would he want her to be

Death Dances at Yuma

there? Could any woman ever share a place in his heart with Holly?

He was brought out of this melancholic thinking by the fleeting sight of three shadows slipping into the camp. Dooley's immediate thought was that they were Apaches, but he dismissed that notion because he had never known Indians to show themselves this far east.

They made their noiseless way to where Kane Prowler lay asleep. Seeing the silhouette of a man pointing a gun down at Prowler, Dooley automatically reached down to his hip with a right hand, but he had left his gunbelt up on the seat of his wagon. That made little difference. His hands were shaking that much he doubted that he would be able to take his six-shooter from its holster.

He had to do something to save the sleeping Prowler. A ray of moonlight glinted off the blade of the long knife that Prowler had left embedded in the root of an oak after cutting kindling for a fire. It was within Dooley's reach. Grasping the handle, he changed his grip to the blade. He came up into a crouch to throw the knife with an expertise that came from years of practice and experience.

The thrown knife thudded into the chest of the man standing above Prowler. Releasing a shot harmlessly, the man crumpled to the ground as Prowler came up out of his bedroll, firing as he came. His bullet slammed into the second man, lifting him off his feet and sending him flying backwards to crash to the ground. The third intruder ran, and the unarmed Dooley rushed to intercept him. They collided heavily, falling to the ground.

Landing on top of Dooley, the man sat back on his heels and drew a Colt.45. Dooley was aware of a once familiar power taking over inside of him. Lashing out with his left foot he kicked his attacker's wrist, sending the .45 spinning out of his hand. Then with his right foot he kicked the man under the chin, snapping back his head. The jawbone broke with a loud splintering sound.

As the man toppled on to his back, Dooley was up on his feet, stamping his right foot hard on the fallen man's throat. Feeling the windpipe and larynx crush wider his foot, Dooley, satisfied that his adversary was dead, was taking a deep breath when a flash from the muzzle of a rifle came from some nearby trees and a bullet plucked at the sleeve of his jacket.

'Dooley!'

Prowler, who was at the wrong angle to tackle the concealed rifleman, shouted Dooley's name and sent a rifle spinning high through the air

Death Dances at Yuma

toward him. Reaching up with his right hand, Dooley deftly plucked the rifle out of the darkness and fired at a gunflash in the trees. A bullet passed close to his face, but a gurgling sound in the trees told him that he had scored a hit.

Dooley felt good. The cold feeling and the sickness had gone. He put his right arm out straight as Prowler walked up. There was not the slightest tremor in his hand.

'Look at that,' he said to Prowler. 'As steady as a rock.'

Slapping him on the back, Prowler said, 'Welcome back to the human race. I told you I could work miracles, Dooley.'

'I don't reckon you can claim credit for this one, Prowler,' Dooley said wryly.

'Probably not. You're good, Dooley, even better than I heard you were.' Prowler stooped to pull the knife out of the dead man's chest. Wiping blood from the blade against his trouser leg, he bent lower to study the corpses. He dismissed the dead men contemptuously. 'Range bums, prepared to kill us for the clothes we stand up in.'

Looking up at the dark sky, Dooley said, 'It'll be getting light in an hour or so, Prowler.'

'That's what I was thinking,' Prowler nodded, still holding the knife. 'Might as well light up a fire, have ourselves some coffee, then get the mules harnessed up. I'll cut us some wood for the fire.'

A determined Dooley objected. 'Leave that to me, Prowler.'

After a moment's hesitation, Prowler suddenly threw the long-bladed knife to Dooley in a swift, underhand movement.

Unmoving as the weapon came directly toward his midriff, Dooley did a short side step at the last moment and unerringly caught the knife by the handle. Prowler had tested him, and he had passed the test. Without a word, Dooley turned and walked away.

When Dooley had the fire going they squatted beside it broiling strips of bacon spitted on mesquite shoots. For the first time in long and depressing ages, Dooley had found himself hungry. Eager to be on the move, he had harnessed the mules to both wagons by the time Prowler had used dregs from the coffee-pot to dowse the fire.

Travelling on they occasionally passed abandoned Apache wickiups along the trail. Only cactus thrived in this wasteland, and some of them stood over fifty feet high. Crossing the brush-covered desert by day, they were aware of smoke signals rising on both sides of the trail.

Pointing at a smoke signal, Prowler asked, 'What are they saying, Dooley?'

'I don't know,' Dooley replied with a shrug. 'No white man can read those signs. The Apache can send information hundreds of miles ahead in less than an hour.'

That night when they had camped, the twinkling of lights in the hills told them that the Indian signals were continuing. Soon after they had started out next morning, Dooley shouted for the wagons to be halted. They were on a rough but serviceable cart trail that led off the Chihuahua Road, and Prowler leapt down from his seat to run back and stand looking up questioningly at Dooley.

'You got a problem, Dooley?'

'*We've* got a problem,' Dooley corrected him.

Bending, Prowler looked along the wagon. 'Something wrong with one of the wheels?'

'That wouldn't be what I'd call a problem,' Dooley answered, as he sprang down effortlessly from the wagon, landing lightly on his feet. All of his old weakness had gone. He pointed to the green splendour of a hillside shrouded in vapours that rose up as the chill rays of the morning sun grew warmer. 'That could be a problem.'

A figure stood beside a horse on the hill. From that distance it was impossible to tell whether the figure was looking down at them. Prowler asked anxiously, 'Apache?'

'Could be,' Dooley acknowledged, walking to the back of his wagon to the buckskin horse that was tied there. Leading the buckskin round, he reached up to take down a rifle from beside the wagon seat. 'I'm going to ride out there to find out what's happening.'

Not pushing his horse, Dooley ascended the slope toward the low mesa. There was something puzzling about the figure that stood as still as a statue. On the mesa he glanced back just once to the sun-drenched valley where an apprehensive and impatient Prowler waited.

Then the figure ahead was close enough to take shape. It was a woman. She was young and tall, even in the moccasins that she wore. Worn loose, her sun-burnished hair flamed over the free-fitting brown dress that she had on. Dooley would have thought her to be an Indian, yet she seemed almost blonde. But the shade darkened to a rich sienna as he rode slowly nearer, leaving him still uncertain.

Part Indian, he decided. Dooley was made wary by the bow in her hand, a hunting arrow notched and ready. As he dismounted, holding his hands out open at each side to indicate that he was no threat to her, she released the bowstring, disarming the long arrow.

There was something primitive about her.

Standing silently, she seemed to blend into the scenery to become a beautiful part of it. She turned her head to him, pointing down to where the wagons and Prowler were tiny in the distance, and asked, 'Who are you and what business do you have on Primeria Alta?'

Three

'I'm Josie Dooley, and the two of us are heading for Fort Yuma,' Dooley answered the girl.

She stood silent and mysterious. Her complexion was deep bronze, either due to race or exposure to the sun. Dooley was still undecided. Taking a brief look westward, she brought her level, dark-eyed gaze back to him. 'I am Juanita.'

'What are you doing out here on the Primeria Alta, the upper frontier, all alone, Juanita?'

The girl again looked westward before turning her head back to study him, not speaking for a long time. Then Dooley read in her eyes that she had decided that she would trust him. That she had no alternative but to trust him.

'I was with a party taking dispatches from the president to the commanding officer at Fort Yuma,' she explained earnestly. 'One of the men got sick along the way and had to be left behind. I stayed with him.'

'Your man?' Dooley enquired, wanting to be sure of the situation.

'A man,' she replied emphatically.

'Where is he, Juanita?'

She pointed west to a group of pines that stood in a small notch among the hills. 'In the shade down there.'

'What's wrong with him?'

'I don't know. He is very sick,' she said, worriedly.

'We'd best go take a look at him,' Dooley said, mounting up, and the girl swung up lithely on to her broomtail horse. The animal was saddled, which meant that she could be no more than part Indian.

Before moving away, Dooley stood in the stirrups to give Prowler an elaborate arm signal that all was well and that he would return soon. Then he followed the girl in a twisting descent down the hill along an almost indiscernible path. Suspicious of the situation, Dooley tensed as they negotiated a narrow defile through some rocks, but they came safely out into the bright open again.

Reaching level ground, Juanita rode to a fallen tree that lay twisted in agonized death.

Dismounting, she hitched her horse to it. Dooley slid out of the saddle and secured the buckskin. He walked warily at her side toward the trees. Suspecting a trap, he held the rifle at the ready.

To signal their approach, Juanita whistled a tune as they walked slowly together. A bird picked her song up joyfully and repeated it. It was echoed distantly but the girl's melody was lost on the counterpoint. She put out an arm against Dooley's chest, slowing hin as they moved into the shadow of the trees. Eyes swiftly adjusting from bright sunlight, he could make out the figure of a man lying in the brush. The right hand of the prone man was resting on his chest, holding a six-shooter. The gun was pointing at Juanita and Dooley.

Working the bolt of his rifle, Dooley was poised to defend himself when the girl called softly to the sick man. 'It's me, Juanita. I have brought help.'

The hand holding the gun slid to one side, and Dooley lowered his rifle to walk in closer. The first thing that struck him was that the ailing man wore neither boots nor socks. Both of his feet were swollen to more than twice their size.

'What is wrong with him?' Juanita asked anxiously.

'Cactus toxin, I guess,' Dooley diagnosed.

'Is there anything you can do for him, Dooley?'

Death Dances at Yuma

'Not a lot.'

A rogue breeze stirred the sick man's thick black hair and Juanita knelt quickly to brush it back. Raising his eyes to look at the man's face for the first time, Dooley was taken aback.

Lying there unconscious, face running with sweat, was Alonzo Corsicana.

'Lieutenant Kearney, ma'am,' the smart young army officer introduced himself. 'In a strange town I always find the saloon the best place to ask questions.'

'I make a living selling liquor not giving information for free, Lieutenant,' Dolores countered. He was lean and handsome, but his obvious vanity irritated her.

She saw Kearney's jaw tighten. There was an urgency about him that was emphasized by the fact that he had left his troop mounted outside of the saloon. Aware of Ace Ormsbie getting up from the card table and strolling casually toward her and the officer, Dolores regretted her flippant reply. Things could turn nasty, and the officer, with his buttoned-down holster high at his waist, wouldn't stand a chance against the gambler.

'Trouble, Miss Dolores?' Ormsbie enquired in his relaxed style.

'This is army business,' Kearney told him.

Death Dances at Yuma

'You involved me the minute you questioned Miss Morelos, Lieutenant.'

'It's all right, Ace,' a frightened Dolores said, before turning to the officer. 'What is it you want to know, Lieutenant Kearney?'

'I'm looking for a man who passed through Mesquite recently with a couple of wagons.'

'There's prairie schooners passing through here regular,' Ormsbie shrugged.

'I'm talking full-sized Conestoga wagons, not schooners,' Kearney said tersely. 'You'd remember this man if you'd seen him. He dresses well, but his face shows what he is. If you saw that face you'd never forget it. He goes by the name of Prowler, Kane Prowler.'

'Never seen nor heard of him.' Ormsbie shook his head.

As the Nevada House relied for its trade on those who lived on the edge of the law and the lawless, the owner and her employees never aided the authorities. Dolores recognized that Ormsbie was following that policy, but worry over Dooley made her break the unwritten rules.

'Could this man have been taking rifles to Fort Yuma, Lieutenant?'

'He's likely to have *said* that's what he was doing,' the officer replied. 'Are you saying that you saw him, Miss Morelos?'

Death Dances at Yuma

Not knowing whether to say more, Dolores looked to Ormsbie for guidance, but the gambler deliberately kept his face averted from her. Taking a deep breath, she answered, 'I think he was in here.'

'When?'

'A few days back.'

'When exactly did he leave Mesquite, Miss Morelos?' Kearney questioned her earnestly.

Hesitating, Dolores tried to get some measure of the officer. She found that his eyes were very hard to read. She said, 'I want something in return if I am to answer that question, Lieutenant.'

'I am a military officer, Miss Morelos,' Kearney told her sternly, 'and I am not authorized to strike bargains. You have a duty to tell me anything that you know about Kane Prowler.'

Dolores nodded. 'I'll tell you, but I want you to know, Lieutenant, that Prowler hired a man from here, Josie Dooley. Whatever you want Prowler for, Dooley has no part in it. He went along with Prowler in good faith.'

'I'll sure keep that in mind, ma'am,' Kearney promised. 'Now tell me when Prowler left here?'

'Three mornings ago.'

'Thank you, Miss Morelos,' the officer said, as he left the saloon hurriedly.

Death Dances at Yuma

'I guess we now know where Prowler got his rifles,' Ormsbie remarked.

'Stolen?' Dolores raised an eyebrow worriedly.

'From the army I'd say.'

Dolores sighed. 'I'm so glad that I told that officer about Dooley.'

'I hate to say it, Dolores,' Ormsbie drawled, 'but I don't reckon that will mean any great shakes when that lieutenant catches up with those two wagons.'

Delirious and with a raging fever, Alonzo Corsicana lay on a blanket that covered ammunition boxes in the rear end of Dooley's wagon. Juanita knelt beside the stricken man, bathing his feet with warm water as Dooley had advised.

Surrounded by hills that were beds of lava topped by chaparral, prickly pear and sand, they were camped at the abandoned Santa Rita copper mine, at the site of the Apache Council Rock. Prowler was cooking a frugal meal over a low fire. The mules, bone thin and fatigued, were grazing grass tight to the ground, while Dooley laboured at greasing the wheels of the two wagons. Using a rock for a fulcrum, he levered up the axle with a length of wood, pushing a larger stone in with his foot as a stand each time before removing a wheel.

Death Dances at Yuma

Though he had complained bitterly when Dooley had brought in the sick man, Prowler had later relented, acknowledging that if the man recovered, then he would be an extra gun along the way to Yuma, and the girl, who was never far from her bow and arrow, looked as if she would prove useful in a fight.

Dooley had told neither Prowler nor Juanita that he knew the man who had been poisoned by cactus needles. He was thinking about Corsicana now as he used grease-covered hands to lubricate an axle stub. If and when he came round, would Corsicana recognize him? What would happen if he did?

Lost in these thoughts as he worked, Dooley saw an alarmed Prowler suddenly stand upright from where he had been hunkering beside the fire. Dooley raised himself up, too, as he saw the small band of mounted Apaches appear. Ponies at a walking pace, they came into the camp. The men in the party were heavily armed with Mexican guns, lances, and bows and arrows; the women were clad in Spanish finery. Dooley knew that the arms and the clothing would have been taken in raids made far to the south.

Young and friendly-looking, the chief dismounted. Waiting respectfully, his sub-chiefs then slid from their ponies to the ground. Wiping the grease from his hands on a piece of sacking, Dooley moved surreptitiously toward where his rifle rested up on the wagon. Even as he walked slowly he realized that it was a pointless exercise. He and Prowler were outnumbered and most certainly outgunned by the Apaches.

The young chief with a hint of a friendly smile on his face, spoke in the Apache language. Unable to understand what the Indian had said, Dooley and Prowler exchanged helpless glances, while Juanita came down from the back of the wagon in a flowing movement, and walked forward gracefully. She carried her bow. The quiver was high on her back, the arrows easily accessible.

Looking at the young chief, but addressing Dooley and Prowler, she translated, 'He says that his name is Joaquis. He wants to be friendly. If you want to be friendly, be will take the presents that you have for him and will let you pass. If not, he and his people are prepared to defend themselves.'

While the girl was speaking, Joaquis stood eyeing her as he waited for her to finish. The Apache chief looked amiable enough, but Dooley was acutely aware of the underlying threat in the request for presents. It had put tension in the air. Unless the Apaches could be appeased they would become belligerent. Once they found the two wagons were carrying rifles and ammunition, Prowler, the girl, the sick man, and Dooley would be killed.

Trying to think of a way out of what, despite a façade of friendliness, was a dire situation, Dooley watched a confident Kane Prowler make a move. His estimation of the man soared as Prowler climbed up into his wagon and brought down a large chest.

Placing the chest on the ground in front of the Apache, he swung the lid open. There were appreciative murmurs from the Indians as Prowler reached into the chest and pulled out his hands full of colourful trinkets. He held them on high, and the women and braves dismounted and came excitedly to the chest.

While his people happily selected trinkets for themselves, Joaquis stood apart from them. Smile fading to be replaced by a frown, the Apache chief was plainly unimpressed by the presents on offer. Aware of this, Dooley was again expecting trouble. But he had again underestimated Prowler, who smilingly held up a hand to Joaquis in a wait-until-you-see-the-gift-that-I-have-for-you sign. Clambering up on to his wagon to reach inside, he jumped back down on to the ground, holding out an Army officer's coat to a delighted Indian chief.

Joaquis put on the jacket. It fitted perfectly, and

he preened himself as his people gathered admiringly around him. Smiling as he strutted up and down in the coat, the Apache chief gave Prowler the peace sign. A watching Dooley was puzzled as to how Prowler could have come by army property.

Dooley said, 'Ask him if he has any mules to trade, Juanita.'

Speaking in Apache to the chief, the girl reported back to Dooley that Joaquis said that he would ask his people if they had any mules to spare. When he had an answer, the Apache chief would meet Prowler and Dooley the next day, ten miles further along the Gila Trail.

Smoothing the soldier's coat he wore with both hands, Joaquis smiled at Prowler and made a speech of some length. A baffled Prowler turned to Juanita to ask, 'What did he say, girl?'

'Joaquis is praising you,' Juanita translated. 'He says that you are the son of the Great White Father. That you are a good friend of his, and that he will protect you and us along the trail.'

'Thank the chief for me, girl, and tell him that I am proud to be his friend.'

Juanita did as Prowler asked, and a nodding Joaquis accepted her words with one of his half-smiles. Then his face became serious as he spoke while beckoning Juanita toward him. Noticing the frown of consternation the Apache's words had caused the girl, Dooley spoke tersely, 'What did he say, Juanita?'

Not turning her head, keeping her steady gaze on the chief, Juanita answered, 'He said that I do not belong with white people. I will make a fine squaw for Joaquis, and that I should leave with him now.'

As this exchange of words was going on, the Apache was looking suspiciously from Juanita to Dooley in turn. The smile had gone. Joaquis' chiselled features were stern and his eyes had hardened.

'Tell him that you are my woman.'

With a gasp, Juanita swung her head to Dooley. 'If I tell him that it will be bad for you, Dooley.'

'Tell him,' Dooley insisted.

Reluctantly, Juanita spoke in Apache and Joaquis replied gutturally. When the chief had finished speaking, the girl looked worriedly at Dooley. 'He says that a good woman is worth fighting for, so it follows that you are ready to fight him to keep me.'

'Back down, Dooley. That's an order,' Prowler called in a voice that had a tremor in it. 'This has been right peaceable, so don't go spoiling it. We need to keep moving to Fort Yuma. The girl's nothing to us so let her go with him.'

Death Dances at Yuma

'She's a human being, Prowler,' Dooley said scathingly, 'and as white men we owe her our protection.'

'I owe her nothing,' a panicking Prowler objected.

Ignoring him, Dooley instructed Juanita, 'Tell him that I am ready to fight to the death to keep my woman.'

'He says that you are a foolish man,' the girl relayed the chief's answer, 'for only a fool would challenge Joaquis, who has never been conquered in any fight. He will leave now, but when we meet tomorrow you must decide whether to let me go or die here on the Gila Trail trying to keep me.'

The Apaches mounted up, and the chief pointed threateningly at Dooley before he wheeled his pony about and led his people away at the same leisurely pace in which they had arrived.

'You've doomed us, Dooley,' an angry Prowler muttered. 'Because of you we will all be dead by this time tomorrow.'

Four

'The horses are tiring fast, sir,' Sergeant Ken Larkin warned respectfully. 'They'll be in poor shape when the going gets tough real soon.'

Lieutenant Matthew Kearney had led his troopers eighteen miles down the Rio Grande at a pace that was hard on the men and rough on their mounts and the pack mules. But he saw himself as having no choice. This was the most urgent and vital mission he had commanded in all of his six years in the army. Though always supremely self-confident, the responsibility of this detail weighed heavily on him. He bore the burden alone, not wanting to worry the sergeant who had become a friend over the years.

'You are right to point that out, Sergeant,' he acknowledged. Larkin, a loyal, experienced and capable soldier, deserved at least a part explana-

Death Dances at Yuma

tion. 'But I have to gamble everything against time. We have to catch up with Prowler before he gets within hollering distance of Yuma.'

'It's that bad, sir?' the sergeant enquired.

'It couldn't be worse, Sergeant,' Kearney replied, tersely. 'We have to take the shortest route, no matter what hardship it entails. Ride back along the column and bring Hueco up here.'

When Larkin wheeled his horse about and left him, the lieutenant kept up the same demanding pace as he continued to follow the river. But he raised an arm to halt the column when the sergeant returned with Hueco, the taciturn Indian guide.

'Tell me how you see it, Hueco,' Kearney said.

Dark face bland, the Indian shrugged as if there was nothing important to be discussed. He asked indifferently, 'What do you want me to tell you, Lieutenant?'

'How to catch up with Kane Prowler, godammit!'

'Well,' Hueco shrugged, 'he's got wagons, so he'll move slower than us.'

'I know that, but he has a three-day start,' the lieutenant snapped.

Remaining silent momentarily, a thoughtful Hueco then said, 'Prowler can take only one route with the wagons, Lieutenant. We have a choice.'

Death Dances at Yuma

'Which route would you choose?' Kearney questioned the Indian sharply.

Tilting his head back, Hueco looked up at the mountains to the right of them. 'There's an old trail up there that only the Indians and the Mexes use.'

'Will it help us make up time, Hueco?'

'Yes, Lieutenant. But it isn't easy.'

'I'm not looking for easy,' Kearney said.

Hueco added another warning in his detached style. 'There's Apaches up there who are as wild as they come, Lieutenant, and Mexican traders who'd slit our throats just to get our boots.'

'All of them are rabble, Hueco,' Kearney said, 'and we are trained soldiers.'

'But we number only thirty, sir,' the sergeant reminded the officer.

'There'll be too many Apaches to count,' Hueco added to Larkin's warning.

Shading his eyes with a raised hand to study the mountains, a worried Larkin sighed. 'Those peaks must be nearly eight thousand feet high, sir.'

'That's not important, Sergeant,' the lieutenant said before turning to the Indian. 'We'll follow your trail, Hueco.'

'Are you sure, sir?' a still doubtful Larkin queried.

Death Dances at Yuma

Arm raised ready to start the column moving, Kearney answered, 'If we don't move fast, Sergeant, there won't be a white man, woman or child left alive west of Phoenix.'

With the faint warmth of a rising sun on his back, Dooley pulled himself up on the tailgate of his wagon. Lying with his eyes closed, Corsicana was looking better. He was no longer feverish, and last night Juanita had reported that the swelling of his feet was going down fast. Satisfied that all was well with the sick man, Dooley had lowered himself to the ground when he heard the Mexican speak.

'I remember you.'

Reaching up with both hands, Dooley resumed his former position to look in the wagon. 'So, what are you saying, Corsicana?'

'I'm saying we left unfinished business back in Tres Piños, Dooley.'

'What mattered in Tres Piños,' Dooley said, 'isn't so important out here on the Gila Trail.'

The Mexican shook his black-haired head slowly. 'Unfinished business is unfinished business.'

'That sounds like a threat to me,' Dooley said.

The Mexican was an additional problem in an already hazardous situation, and Dooley regretted bringing him back to the wagons. At the speed he was recovering, Corsicana would soon be fit and dangerous. His reputation as a fearless gunfighter was widespread. Knowing that a decision needed to be made about the Mexican there and then, Dooley was forced to pause as Prowler looked round the back of the wagon. His manner was shifty. He jerked back quickly, and Dooley went after him.

'Is something wrong, Prowler?' he called.

Walking away, Prowler looked over his shoulder to say, 'Not really.'

'That's a half answer,' Dooley objected, aware that something was amiss.

Taking in all of the small camp in one sweeping gaze, Dooley made a swift mental inventory. Then it came to him. Juanita's broomtail horse was missing! Running to catch up with Prowler he put a hand on the stocky man's muscle-packed shoulder to spin him round. Prowler reacted angrily.

'You won't get away with laying a hand on me twice, Dooley.'

Ignoring the menace in Prowler's statement, Dooley asked urgently, 'Where's the girl?'

'Around some place, I guess,' Prowler replied casually, glancing around as if expecting to see Juanita appear at any moment.

'Come off it, Prowler. Her horse has gone.'

Dooley knew that Prowler was hiding something.

'Then it seems like she lit out in the night,' Prowler admitted grudgingly. 'She was one of them, Dooley. Purty enough, I grant you, but a savage all the same. Call of the wild got to her I reckon.'

Dooley knew different. The girl had ridden off to surrender herself to Joaquis to stop the showdown with Dooley that the Apache chief had threatened for later that day. She had come to Dooley last night, backlit by a golden sunset, standing looking at him as if she had much to say. But she had said nothing, except when she had turned to walk away. Her softly spoken words had been barely audible on the thin air of late evening:

'You are a fine man, Josie Dooley.'

Now, determined not to allow Juanita to sacrifice herself for him, Dooley dashed to the back of his wagon. Corsicana jerked up into a sitting position, but Dooley ignored him. Pulling his saddle from the wagon, he ran to his horse with it on his shoulder.

He had the buckskin saddled and was straightening up after tightening the girth when Prowler strode up to him aggressively. He stood for a moment, watching Dooley buckle on his gunbelt.

'What you got in mind, Dooley?'

'I'm going to fetch the girl back.'

Death Dances at Yuma

Prowler wagged his head from side to side. 'You're wrong there, mister. Unsaddle that horse and we'll get started on the trail. You agreed to get these rifles to Yuma with me. You forget that I own that horse, I own that saddle, and I own these wagons.'

'But you don't own me.'

'That's a matter of opinion,' a cold-eyed Prowler drawled. 'Seems like I recall you being the saloon bum in Mesquite before I came along.'

'Go strap on your gunbelt, Prowler, and we'll settle what's between us right now.'

'No. We'll settle it one day, Dooley, you can be certain of that, but not now,' Prowler said, before turning on his heel and walking away.

Watching him go for a brief second, Dooley then swung up into the saddle and headed for the hills.

Their first night in the mountains was black. Clouds obscured the sky and Kearney had his sergeant double the guard throughout the hours of darkness. The lieutenant was expecting trouble. Before daylight had failed the previous evening, Hueco had discovered the indistinct trail of a fairly large body of horsemen while scouting up ahead. For some reason the tracks had diverted from the trail, but Hueco was convinced that the body of several hundred horsemen was

Death Dances at Yuma

headed in the direction of Kearney's camp. Now there was an air of expectancy about the military detachment. The troopers not on guard duty lay exhausted but uneasy on thick layers of spruce and cedar boughs.

The night passed without incident. But when the next day dawned calm and foggy and the camp was astir, a sentry hurried in to report to Kearney that a mounted party was approaching. With his troop on full alert, Lieutenant Kearney couldn't conceal his embarrassment from his men when he found himself facing nothing more dangerous than a small band of Mexican traders driving a herd of some 500 unbroken horses.

Unnerved at finding themselves facing a line of uniformed riflemen, the Mexican party halted uncertainly. An elderly, sallow-faced man was apparently the leader, and he urged his jaded black pony slowly on to stop in front of Kearney.

Pushing a sombrero thick with alkali dust back from his forehead, the Mexican announced, 'I am Pedro Sanchez, Señor Lieutenant.'

'What is your business on the Gila Trail, Sanchez?' Kearney asked.

Gesturing to where his little band of men was circling the unbroken horses to keep them herded together, Sanchez answered, 'I am taking these many horses from California to Sonora, *señor*. We are peaceable people, Lieutenant, just simple traders and not *bandidos*.'

Accepting this with a nod, the lieutenant enquired, 'Have you seen any wagons along the trail?'

'Two,' Sanchez reported, 'but we saw them only from a great distance, *señor*. I fear they will go little further.'

'Why do you say that?'

'A band of Apaches watch the two wagons constantly from the hills, Señor Lieutenant, and El Toro is coming along the Gila Trail toward the wagons.'

'Who is El Toro, Sanchez?'

'El Toro is *mal hombre*, a very bad man, Señor Lieutenant,' the old Mexican replied, 'a bandit leader, murderer, rustler, and horse thief.'

Exchanging worried glances with his sergeant, Kearney enquired, 'How many men ride with this El Toro, Sanchez?'

'Only five this time, Señor Lieutenant, but they are killers and carry many guns.'

Perturbed by this information, Kearney allowed the Mexicans to continue on their way, and then called Ken Larkin to one side. They walked up an easy slope together until what the lieutenant had to say couldn't be heard by the troopers.

Death Dances at Yuma

'What Sanchez says makes it necessary for us to move faster, Sergeant.'

'The men are tough, sir, fine soldiers,' Larkin said, 'but the animals are in poor shape. We try to put packs on the mules right now and most of them will collapse.'

'Nevertheless, we have to move out, and move fast, Sergeant. We have to make sure that those two wagons get to Fort Yuma.'

'I don't understand, sir,' a puzzled sergeant said, furrowing his brow. 'Aren't our orders to arrest Prowler and confiscate his wagons and the stolen rifles?'

Placing a friendly hand on his sergeant's shoulder, Kearney apologized. 'It's not like that, Sergeant, and I am sorry that I haven't explained it to you before now. Prowler isn't taking the rifles to Fort Yuma. He has arranged to meet an Apache chief called Galvez Chama just this side of the Fort.'

'And sell him the rifles,' Larkin gasped.

'Exactly,' the lieutenant confirmed. 'Galvez Chama is leading an Apache uprising. He needs those rifles and has the gold to pay well for them.'

'With those rifles, sir, the Apaches will massacre every white person in the territory, the military included.'

Nodding agreement, Kearney said, 'That is why

Death Dances at Yuma

we have to time it right. We have to take Prowler and the wagons shortly before he is due to meet the Apache chief. That way we wreck the plan by escorting Prowler and the wagons into safety at Fort Yuma. So we can't allow a different band of Apaches or a Mexican gang to take the rifles off Prowler out here on the trail. If that happened we wouldn't be able to control the situation.'

'I'll get the troop moving, sir,' the earnest sergeant said, as he saluted and hurried away.

Fording a murky stream that was not quite large enough for his horse to swim, Josie Dooley rode down a talus that led to where the band of Apaches had camped for the night. A thick, watery fog lay over the mountains, but the Indians would be aware of his approach. They had probably been watching him from way back.

Some women going about their chores glanced sullenly in his direction as he rode in. Children filled with curiosity gathered to stare at him through huge black eyes. Braves showing no signs of aggression lingered on the sidelines, ready to wait to see whether he came in peace or seeking trouble. It was a temporary camp. The Apaches had broken brush and branches to build shelters into which they had crawled with their feet toward fires on what must have been a cold night up high.

Death Dances at Yuma

Looking for Juanita, Dooley showed no reaction when she stepped out from a group of squaws, her haughty head held high. There was no way that he could tell how she felt about him having come after her. Juanita's high-cheekboned face was inscrutable, and it remained that way even when Joaquis appeared to stand squarely in front of Dooley's advancing horse. The Apache was bare to the waist, the sheen on his bronze skin enhancing the superb muscularity of his body.

Reining up, Dooley dismounted slowly. Moving his horse to one side, he faced the Apache chief with just a few feet separating them. Joaquis pointed to Dooley's gunbelt, saying something in his own language.

In a flat tone, Juanita translated what the chief had said. 'You have no need of a gun here. You must take off your belt and hand it to me.'

Unbuckling the belt without taking his eyes from Joaquis, Dooley wrapped it around the holstered gun and passed it to the girl. Taking it, Juanita started to say something, but a grunted word of warning coming from the chief stopped her.

Smiling, Joaquis reached behind himself to pull a wide-bladed knife from his waistband. Still smiling, he tossed the knife from hand to hand. Without warning, he threw the knife high over his head; the sun glinting off the blade as it twisted and twirled. The knife came spinning down behind him, and the Apache chief put a hand back to catch it deftly, then sent it spinning up high again from behind his back, to catch the weapon as it came down in front of him.

In another sudden move, Joaquis threw the knife and the blade thudded into the ground between Dooley's feet. Not flinching, Dooley calmly stooped to grasp the handle and pull the knife from the sod. Straightening up, Dooley did exactly the same throwing and spinning act with the knife as the Apache had. Not in the least intimidated, Joaquis seemed pleased by Dooley's show of dexterity. Reaching to his waistband behind him, the Apache produced an identical knife. Beckoning forward a sub chief who held a strip of rawhide in his hands, the Apache chief began talking, with Juanita translating.

'Orto will lash our left wrists together, Dooley, and will signal for the fight to start. This woman is special which demands that we fight to the death. Orto has his orders. If you should win he is to cut you free from me and no one will prevent you from riding off with the woman.'

With a nod to say that he understood, Dooley extended his left arm for the sub chief to tie the wrist to Joaquis. The Apache was a fine physical

Death Dances at Yuma

specimen, and Dooley recognized that he faced a formidable opponent. As the chief's muscular arm came against his, Dooley realized what had put the shine on the Indian's skin. Joaquis was coated in bear grease, which would make his body so slippery it would be impossible to get a hold on him.

Looking toward Juanita, who avoided his gaze, Dooley fretted over her fate should he lose this fight. The odds were certainly stacked against him. Resigned to whatever was to happen, Dooley heard the sub chief bark out a command and he felt the rawhide dig into his wrist as Joaquis pulled on his arm. A fight to the death had begun.

Five

Lieutenant Matthew Kearney had lost his gamble to cover the greatest distance in the shortest time. Keeping up a relentless pace over difficult terrain had taken a toll on both the men and the animals. His exhausted, bedraggled soldiers were now afoot most of the time to spare horses that were in a terrible condition. The mules laboured on under their burdens, but were in imminent danger of collapse. Even the tough Sergeant Larkin looked worn and haggard. Kearney, in spite of his military training and discipline and his self-confidence as an officer, felt increasing despair. For the first time in his military career he was in command of a mission doomed to failure. The possibility of catching up with Prowler was diminishing by the minute. Supplies had run worryingly low, and Heuco had warned that they faced an immediate twelve-day march with scarcely any grazing for the animals.

Late on an afternoon when they had sighted Casa Montezuma, their luck seemed to have changed when the Indian guide rode back with some good news. Up ahead the Pima Indians were coming out from their villages to meet them.

'What does that mean, Heuco?' a weary Kearney questioned. 'The men are in no condition to get into a fight.'

Dismissing this with a shake of his head, the Indian replied, 'They are an agricultural people, sir. The Pima raise cotton, corn and beans in abundance, and they have fine horses and mules. They are eager to trade food and cattle.'

When he had moved his men forward steadily and at last met the Pima Indians, Kearney was shocked. Unlike the proud, athletic and graceful Apache, these people were dull-faced. Both men and women were naked from the waist upwards. The men seemed sly, and the women were without exception ugly. But they lived well. Their land was fenced and well irrigated, and their homes were thatched mud huts. The most important sight for Kearney was that of the Indians' fine horses and mules.

'Tell them we are prepared to trade, Heuco, and will pay well for meal and flour,' the lieutenant

Death Dances at Yuma

ordered his guide. 'But concentrate on buying as many horses and mules as they are willing to part with.'

Heuco's voice rose and fell as he haggled with the Pima Indians. There was much arm waving between him and the Indians, and short bursts of scornful laughter when a price considered extortionate was suggested, or a too low offer was made. He walked back to Kearney to report on the deals he had struck. 'I've got food supplies cheaper than you could buy them in a Santa Fe store, sir, but they know what their cattle are worth, and won't go below ten dollars a head.'

'Then pay them what they are asking,' Kearney said, keen to replenish his detail and get on the move once more. 'What about horses and mules?'

The Indian guide shuffled his feet in discomfort. 'We're out of luck there, sir. The Pima say their horses and mules aren't up for trade.'

'But they have to be, Heuco. Horses and mules are what we need most of all.'

'They won't part with even one animal, and there's no way that I can change their mind,' the Indian said.

Shoulders slumping in disappointment, Kearney turned to Larkin. 'Where does that leave us, Sergeant?'

'In a whole heap of trouble, sir.'

'Heuco?' the lieutenant asked, ready to consider all suggestions.

'Well,' the guide began contemplatively, 'the Pima won't sell them, but there's enough troopers here to shoot all the Indian folk down and take the horses and mules that we need.'

'I'm an army officer, not some Mexican leading a bandit gang.' Kearney rebuked Heuco. Pausing in thought for few minutes, he came to a decision. He spoke to Ken Larkin. 'We're going to have to remain here and have the men rest and let what horses and mules we have left recuperate. How long do you estimate, Sergeant – two days?'

'I would recommend three days, sir, to be sure of a result,' the sergeant replied. Anxious about the lead that Prowler was gaining on them, and having to accept that the Apaches and the Mexican El Toro might well have raided the wagons already, Kearney started to insist on a rest of no more than two days' duration. Then he remembered that his haste had already lost them valuable time. He gave a grudging nod of assent:

'Three days, Sergeant, and not a half a day longer. Have the men make camp.'

Within seconds of Orto signalling for the fight to begin, Dooley made two daunting discoveries. The first was that Joaquis possessed unbelievable

Death Dances at Yuma

strength, and the second was that his own recovery had been superficial. Though he could respond instantly and effectively to an emergency, his response couldn't be sustained. Years of an inadequate diet and heavy drinking had seriously weakened him inwardly. Now an overall light sweat had quickly grown cold on his skin and he felt so unwell that his limbs were without power. With Joaquis eager for the kill, Dooley circled, keeping as much distance from the Apache chief as their tied wrists would permit.

An absence of aggression in his opponent appeared to promote a lack of interest in Joaquis. A bored expression on his face, the Apache relaxed his body and looked around at his people. He was showing his disappointment and silently apologizing for the poor opposition. All too late, Dooley recognized this as a ploy. With a speed that caught Dooley off balance, Joaquis yanked on his left arm to pull him in close. At the same time the knife in the Apache's right came sweeping up, the wide blade aimed at Dooley's solar plexus.

Practically defenceless, Dooley used the force as he collided with Joaquis to turn his body a little. Missing its target, the knife sliced through Dooley's side. He felt steel grate against his ribs, and was aware of blood gushing from the wound. The sight and scent of blood brought the savage in

Joaquis surging to the fore. Keeping Dooley tight against him, he went for his throat with a cross-body slashing movement of the knife.

All Dooley could do was pull his own head against his chest to protect his throat. The tip of the Apache's razor-sharp knife travelled across his forehead, digging hard against the bone as it went and opening up a flap of skin from one side of Dooley's head to the other.

Enfeebled by the loss of blood from his side, Dooley now had to cope with blood from his head wound running stickily and stingingly into his eyes. Almost blinded by this, Dooley attempted to back away. But Joaquis stayed in close to him, and the watching, usually impassive Apaches, were now howling and hollering for the kill.

Swaying sideways within the tight limits allowed him, Dooley avoided another knife thrust to the chest. This time the blade skidded across his shoulder, the wound it inflicted neither deep nor serious.

But a desperate Dooley was starkly aware that it was only a matter of time, a very short time, before the Apache delivered a fatal blow. In his weak state he had been no match for the powerful Joaquis to begin with, but now he was almost as helpless as a baby. He reasoned that he had perhaps enough strength in reserve for just one effective movement. But, with defeat staring him in the face, what possible move could he make that would be decisive?

Deriving enjoyment from delaying the kill, Joaquis turned round and round on the spot, pulling on Dooley who had to keep running and stumbling in a dizzying circle. Bleeding profusely from his head and side, disoriented by a flap of skin from his forehead hanging over his eyes, giddiness made it difficult for Dooley to keep his feet. He took a wild swipe at the Apache, but was hopelessly out of range and his knife cut only through air. But the attempt angered Joaquis, and he stopped playing with Dooley and moved to finish him off.

As the Apache's knife came at him once more in an arc with the intent of disembowlment, Dooley made a split-second decision. Taking a short step forward so that Joaquis was slightly behind him, Dooley summoned up every scrap of strength and energy available in his damaged body. Keeping his left arm tight against him, he suddenly did a lightning backward somersault.

The unsuspecting Apache chief's left arm, bound tightly to Dooley's at the wrist, was away from his body. It was twisted by the somersault, and as Dooley landed on his feet he was half-deafened by Joaquis' scream of agony as his left arm was wrenched from its socket at his shoulder.

Death Dances at Yuma

Catching the Apache while he was still in great pain, Dooley used his knife for the first time in the fight. In a backhanded slashing movement, he opened up a gash in Joaquis' neck, severing the jugular. The Apache's lifeblood spewed out, rising high like a spluttering, splattering red fountain.

Though he knew that Joaquis was dead as the Apache sank to the ground, something in Dooley had him make sure by stabbing his erstwhile opponent in the belly and jerking the knife upward to open up the bronze body like a carcass.

Being tied to Joaquis, Dooley collapsed on top of the corpse. Still bleeding freely himself, he was aware that his blood was mingling with that of the dead Apache. Blood brothers, Dooley thought ludicrously and wanted to laugh. But a creeping blackness filled his head.

When he half regained consciousness, Orto, the Apache sub chief, was cutting through the throng that bound his wrist to the dead Joaquis. Juanita was kneeling beside him, pressing pads of folded material against the wounds in his head and side. Dooley saw this in a haze, then he blacked out again.

Fretting over being delayed, Prowler had waited a full twenty-four hours for Dooley's expected return. Not prepared to wait longer, he had a much-improved Corsicana drive Dooley's wagon, and moved out. On an easy stretch of the trail they made ten miles, and would have gone further but the iron tyre came off one of the wheels of Prowler's wagon.

'It's lucky that we're beside this creek,' Prowler remarked, as he and Corsicana laboured to remove the wagon wheel.

'Why's that?' the Mexican asked, puzzled. 'I know nothing about wagons, Prowler.'

'We'll need water to shrink the tyre on to the wheel,' Prowler answered. 'Gather plenty of brushwood together, Corsicana. We need a big fire.'

When they had the fire going, Prowler went to his wagon and brought back two crowbars. Passing one to Corsicana, he instructed him to hook the end of the bar under the iron rim. Across the tyre from the Mexican, Prowler did the same and together they lifted it into the fire.

'Now we wait until it's red hot,' Prowler said.

A lot of the brushwood they had used for the fire was green, and a column of smoke rose thick and high into the air. Corsicana looked at it worriedly. 'That will let anyone within a hundred miles know where we're at, Prowler.'

'It can't be helped,' Prowler shrugged. 'We've got to take that chance. I need to get these wagons to Fort Yuma fast.'

Death Dances at Yuma

Staying silent while he rolled and lit a cigarette, the Mexican then casually strolled to Prowler's wagon to take the rifle down from the seat and stand it against the nearest of the remaining three wheels. Having watched him uneasily, Prowler tersely asked a question.

'What's that for?'

'In case we attract visitors,' the Mexican explained, drawing his six-shooter from its tied-down holster and spinning the chamber to check that it was fully loaded.

Dropping the gun back into its holster, the young gunman came to stand beside Prowler to watch the iron tyre change colour in the fire. He spoke in a conversational way.

'I know what you're carrying to Yuma, Prowler.'

'So?'

'I'd say that the two wagonloads will fetch a fair sum of money.'

'That's my business,' Prowler said coldly.

'That's the truth,' Corsicana agreed with a nod. 'But it seems to me that you'd have a problem getting two wagons to Yuma all on your lonesome.'

'Dooley will be back.'

'Reckon he will,' the Mexican nodded. 'But then again maybe he won't.'

Looking at Corsicana from the corners of his eyes, Prowler said, 'I'll be straight with you,

Death Dances at Yuma

Corsicana. If Dooley gets back, then I'll pay him his share at the end of the trail. If he don't, then you get that wagon there for me and you can have Dooley's share. Now, take up that iron. We've got to get that tyre out of the fire.'

Prowler had the wooden wheel lying flat on the ground. Together they lifted the glowing red iron tyre from the fire and fitted it exactly over the wooden rim. Then, on Prowler's instructions, they struggled with the wheel to the creek and tossed it in. There was a loud hissing and steam drifted up like a fog.

'That's it,' a satisfied Prowler exclaimed.

Standing together in the creek, they lifted the wheel upright. The tyre had shrunk tightly on it, and they rolled it out of the water and over to the wagon.

Working with Prowler to replace the wheel on the axle, Corsicana said quietly, 'Whether Dooley comes back or he doesn't, I'll be taking his share of the money at Yuma, Prowler.'

'That's between you and Dooley, son.'

'That's right,' the Mexican concurred. 'Me and Dooley go back aways, Prowler. There's something between us that has to be settled.'

Straightening up, the wheel now secure on the wagon, Prowler wiped grease from his hands. 'As I said, Corsicana, it's between you and Josie

Death Dances at Yuma

Dooley. But you and Dooley aren't going to interfere with the deal I got going here. If he comes back, *compadre*, I won't let you settle anything between you until we reach Yuma.'

'You have my word on that, Prowler,' Corsicana declared, he held out his right hand. 'Shake on it.'

Not taking the proffered hand, Prowler spoke chillingly, 'I never shake the hand of a man I might have to kill.'

Accepting this with a straight-lipped smile, the Mexican's eyes widened as he looked over Prowler's shoulder. He spoke urgently. 'We have company, *amigo*.'

Turning to see five horsemen slowly approaching in line, Prowler identified their race. 'Mexes. They're your people, Corsicana. Do you know them?'

'I know them. That's El Toro and some of his men,' a grim-faced Corsicana answered. 'This is bad, Prowler.'

Hand going inside of his coat to his shoulder holster, Prowler's eyes flicked to where the Mexican had propped the rifle against the wheel of the wagon. He asked hissingly from the side of his mouth, 'Can you get to my rifle, son?'

'We can't make any kind of move, Prowler,' Corsicana advised. 'El Toro could hit a woodtick on a rock at three hundred yards.

Death Dances at Yuma

The five horsemen reined up. The man in the centre had a broad grin on his heavy, dark-complexioned face. The riders flanking him wore solemn expressions. All five held rifles across the saddle in front of them in a relaxed but nevertheless threatening manner.

The bandit leader's gaze took in the dying fire and the blackened wheel on the wagon. His white teeth flashed. 'El Toro is always willing to help Americanos, *amigos*. But, sadly, we arrive too late.'

'We thank El Toro for his kindness,' Prowler said, 'but the wagon is now fixed and we are ready to roll.'

'What is your hurry, *amigo*?' El Toro enquired, with a gurgling laugh. He pointed to the north. 'Whether you go north, or' – he pointed west – 'to the west, or' – he pointed south – 'south, or' – he pointed east – 'to the east, you are a long way from anywhere.'

'We have to get moving,' Prowler insisted.

El Toro dismounted and walked toward Prowler's wagon, carrying his rifle in one hand.

'If that is so, *señor*, your prairie schooners must carry very valuable cargo. Maybe El Toro should escort you.'

Both Prowler and Corsicana tensed, and the four mounted Mexicans brought their rifles up to cover them. El Toro leaned his rifle against the wagon and climbed up to look inside. He stayed looking inside for some time. Dropping back down to the ground, he picked up his rifle and, still smiling, held it waist high aimed at Prowler.

'I now understand your hurry, *amigo*, and El Toro is willing to help you,' the bandit leader said. 'You and your *compadre* can travel light and fast. Me and my men will take these wagons from you.'

'I can't let you do that, El Toro,' Kane Prowler said firmly, fearlessly meeting and holding the Mexican bandit's gaze.

Giving emphasis to his words with a jerk of the rifle he was holding, El Toro chuckled. 'A dead man cannot stop me, *compadre*.'

Six

Josie Dooley became hazily conscious. When the mists cleared from his mind, he saw that he was inside of a makeshift shelter. Juanita was kneeling beside him, her arm under his head, her anxious face close to his. His forehead was raging with a close to unbearable pain. It was really a series of sharp pains that were caused by an elderly squaw who knelt at his head. Grunting with each move she made, she was employing some painful method of clamping the skin of his forehead back together. Dooley could feel that though his side had been bound tightly, it was hurting.

There was a lot of singing and dancing going on outside, interrupted every now and then by ear-splitting yells. Remembering that Joaquis was dead and that he had killed him, Dooley wondered whether the Apaches were mourning one dead chief or choosing another. The alternative was that the singing and dancing was in preparation for revenge, which would mean that they would be coming for him. That didn't fit in with compassion shown by having the squaw tend his wounds, but maybe it was Juanita who had achieved that short-term amnesty.

'It's all right,' Juanita whispered soothingly, when she saw that his eyes were open. 'Lie still. It is nearly done.'

'Why are they dancing?' he asked hoarsely.

'They are preparing to select a new chief. A young buck named Tumacacoro has challenged Orto,' Juanita explained. She added fearfully, 'Tumacacoro is dangerous, Josie. If the Apaches choose him, then I don't think we'll ever get out of here.'

'It looks like I'll have to fight another Apache chief,' Dooley said, his voice faint from weakness and pain.

Shaking her head, Juanita dismissed the idea. 'You cannot fight in your condition. It would be of no use anyway, as all the young braves favour Tumacacoro as chief. You kill him and they will kill you. Many of them already want you dead because you killed Joaquis.'

'It looks as if we're in trouble.'

'I'm sorry,' she apologized humbly. 'I got you into this.'

Death Dances at Yuma

'No,' Dooley argued. 'Riding in after you was my choice.'

'Why did you come after me, Josie?'

A frown creased Juanita's bronze forehead as, avidly, she awaited his response. But Dooley didn't know the answer to her question. Unable to reply, he remained silent.

The squaw had completed her work on his head and the pain was receding a little. She poured a thick liquid into a bowl and passed it to Juanita, who in turn held it out to Dooley.

'Drink this.'

The drink was bitter and foul tasting, but it had an almost immediate rejuvenating effect. With Juanita's assistance, Dooley got up first into a sitting position. It took a while for his head to stop swimming. When the giddiness had abated, his balance was faulty and his limbs wouldn't obey him properly as, with an effort, he crawled out of the shelter and Juanita helped him get shakily to his feet.

Able to stand with the aid of an arm round Juanita's shoulders, Dooley took in the scene. The braves were dancing, whooping and yelling, while Orto stood face to face with a heavily muscled, aggressive Apache who, Dooley assumed, was Tumacacoro. To the left of Juanita and himself, a small group of elders sat cross-legged on the

Death Dances at Yuma

ground. Their old faces lined, they were in full ceremonial dress and one of them stretched an arm to point at Dooley and speak gutturally.

'What did he say?' Dooley asked Juanita.

'That you beat Joaquis in a fair fight, and the Apaches will be forever dishonoured if we are not allowed to leave.'

It was plain to Dooley that the younger Indians didn't share this sentiment. They stopped dancing and gathered round the two prospective chiefs as Tumacacoro raised his voice angrily at Orto who stood calmly, saying nothing. It was turning nasty, and with Orto being of a much lighter build than his adversary, Dooley doubted that he would have a lot of chance against Tumacacoro.

In a swift movement that caught Orto and the spectators by surprise, Tumacacoro turned his back on Orto. Reaching behind with his powerful right arm, Tumacacoro gripped Orto round the neck. Bending forward and pulling at the same time, he threw Orto. Dooley was impressed when Orto landed on his back on the ground in front of Tumacacoro. He saw the way that Orto saved his body from shock by slapping the ground simultaneously with the soles of his feet and the palms of his hands as he hit the earth. Orto knew his stuff. He was a fighting man.

Tumacacoro moved in as Orto came up on to all

Death Dances at Yuma

fours. But Orto impressed Dooley even more by staying bent over as he ran forward a few steps to thrust his head between Tumacacoro's legs. As his shoulders crashed against the front of Tumacacoro's thighs, Orto suddenly stood up, throwing Tumacacoro with such force that he did one and a half somersaults through the air before slamming heavily to the ground.

Now the young braves were yelling for Orto to finish it. His skill as a fighter had won them over. Then there was a concerted roar of shock and disapproval as Tumacacoro, still flat on his back, grasped a stone and hurled it viciously at Orto. Catching Orto on the brow, the stone split the skin above the eye and knocked him off his feet.

Scrambling up, Tumacacoro struggled to pick up a huge rock. Muscles bulging, he lifted the rock high above his head in both hands and took a few stiff-legged steps to stand over the fallen Orto. Conscious but unable to move, Orto looked up helplessly as Tumacacoro let out a mighty roar and readied himself to send the massive rock down on his dazed opponent. All of the watching Apaches were silent. The cheating Tumacacoro was about to kill Orto, and they were sickened by the cowardly act.

With even the elders sitting mute, Dooley had been waiting for at least one Indian to come to

Death Dances at Yuma

Orto's rescue. Able to delay no longer, he took his arm from Juanita's shoulders and tested both his strength and balance. Neither passed the test, but with no choice he did a staggering run toward Tumacacoro. Stumbling twice, he kept on to come up behind the Apache and throw himself the last few feet.

Dooley's right shoulder crashed against the back of Tumacacoro's knees. The Apache fell backwards, releasing his two-handed hold on the rock. Making an avoiding roll to one side on the ground, Dooley heard what sounded like an explosion as the heavy boulder landed on Tumacacoro's head, bursting it open.

Avoiding looking at the jagged edges of the Apache's broken skull and the blood and brains that were spattered over the ground, Juanita ran to Dooley. With Orto's assistance, she got him to his feet. The Apache was saying something, and Juanita repeated it in English for Dooley.

'A boy has our horses ready for us, Josie. Orto says that he is now chief, but he can't guarantee our safety until his people have settled down. We must go at once. Can you ride?'

Knees giving way, Dooley could tell that the wound in his forehead had opened up. He could feel warn blood pouring from it, and there was a trickle of blood running down into his right eye.

Death Dances at Yuma

Slamming into Tumacacoro must have undone some of the good work the squaw had done on his head.

'I can ride,' he told Juanita, but neither she nor he believed it.

Orto helped her get Dooley up into the saddle, but the small effort that he'd personally had to make was too much for him. As Dooley slumped forward against the neck of his horse, Orto placed a hand on his leg and said something. With a pleased smile on her face, Juanita was about to translate when she realized that Dooley wouldn't be able to hear her.

Up in the saddle, she took the reins of Dooley's horse and led it and its unconscious rider out of the Apache camp.

The sun rose up from behind the mountains, clearing away the shadows from the Pima Indian village as the soldiers listlessly broke camp. Kearney's detail was in a bad way. The men had benefitted from the long rest and plenty of food, but several of the mules had died. Those left were, like the horses, too far gone to recover fully. His troopers lacked enthusiasm for the trail ahead, and Kearney himself was too dejected to make any attempt at rallying their spirits. The vital mission to capture Kane Prowler and the rifles he was transporting now seemed doomed.

Both the officer and his men were lethargically going through the motions of preparation for going back on the trail, when Heuco came riding back in. Not dismounting, the Indian scout wheeled his horse to rein up beside Kearney and lean over in the saddle to speak to him.

'There's a company of soldiers heading our way, sir.'

Looking up at Heuco in disbelief, a bewildered lieutenant asked an unnecessary question. 'Are you sure?'

'If I made mistakes, Lieutenant, you would have been dead years ago.'

'Forgive me, Heuco,' Kearney said to placate the Indian. 'It's just that there should be no other army units in this territory.'

'Looks to me like they're from the Mormon Battalion, sir,' the scout said. Sitting upright in the saddle he held his head on one side. 'Listen!'

Listening, Kearney at first heard nothing, and then coming to him faintly was a choir of male voices singing 'The Girl I Left Behind Me'.

As the singing grew louder, Kearney and his men ceased their task and stood watching as a double column of cavalry rode up with a captain at the head. The men of the company were

Death Dances at Yuma

smartly uniformed. Their horses were in excellent condition, as were the spare horses and mules that brought up the rear.

Approaching middle age, the captain was tall in the saddle. He looked with surprise and then compassion at the poor state of Kearney's detail. Raising his arm to halt the company behind him, the captain dismounted and marched smartly across to Kearney, who came to attention and saluted him.

'Captain Arnold Blake, Lieutenant,' the senior officer said as he returned the salute.

'Lieutenant Matthew Kearney, Captain.'

Looking around him, Blake observed sympathetically, 'You would seem to be in a bad way, Lieutenant Blake. I assume that you, too, are heading back to Santa Fe?'

'I'm afraid not, sir. We are bound for Fort Yuma.'

Blake made a clicking sound with his tongue. 'My word, Lieutenant! Even if we discount the Apaches and the Mexicans and the natural hazards of the Gila Trail, your detail is in no fit state to make it to Fort Yuma.'

With a shrug, Kearney said, 'My orders are to reach Yuma, Captain Blake. A lot depends on us getting there.'

Taking off his leather gloves, Blake held both in one hand, slapping them against his thigh as he bowed his head in thought. Then, with a resolute expression on his face, he looked up at Kearney. 'In that case, Lieutenant Kearney, and as we only have to make for Santa Fe, I will supply you with both fresh mounts and mules.'

'But. . . .' Kearney was taken aback. 'What of army rules and regulations, Captain?'

Captain Blake gave him a wry smile. 'What of them? I am making a decision in the field, and will argue justification for that decision if needs be.'

'In my position I would be foolish to refuse, Captain, but it is you who will face the consequences if I accept.'

'Leave me to worry about that, Matthew,' the captain advised. 'I am a Mormon first and a soldier second. When the Mormon Battalion was formed and gathered at Council Bluffs, Brigham Young gave us our instructions from the church. I remember it word for word: "Let no man go without his garment and always wear a coat and vest; keep neat and clean, teach chastity, gentility and civility; swearing must not be admitted; insult no man; have no contentious conversation with the Missourian, Mexican, or any class of people; do not preach, only where people desire to hear, and then be wise men. Impose not your principles on any people . . . never trespass on the rights of others . . . should the battalion engage with the enemy and be successful, treat prisoners with the greatest civility, and never take life if it can be avoided".

'If I were to allow you to continue while handicapped so badly as you now are, Matthew, then I would be taking the lives of you and your men when it could be avoided.'

'God bless you, Captain,' Kearney said.

'I do hope that He will, Matthew,' Arnold Blake remarked, with another of his wry smiles. 'Now, tell me your needs and I will have my men pass over whatever you need.'

Turning from the captain, Kearney called. 'Sergeant Larkin!'

'Sir,' the sergeant responded, as he came up smartly and saluted.

'Make a list of what we need to get us to Fort Yuma, Sergeant; supplies, mules, and horses.'

When Kearney's bedraggled soldiers heard this they shrugged off despondency. Their backs straightened, their shoulders squared and, despite being a disciplined force, they spontaneously voiced a cheer.

Nonchalantly leaning a shoulder against Prowler's wagon, El Toro's face wore the crazed grin of a man who killed for pleasure. Finger tightening on the trigger of a rifle pointed at Prowler's chest, he used a movement of his head to give his four mounted men a close to imperceptible signal that they were to blast Corsicana.

'Hold on, El Toro,' Prowler said hoarsely. 'It doesn't have to be like this. I reckon as how we can do a deal on the rifles.'

His grin broadening, El Toro had a chuckle in his voice as he replied., 'You are not offering a deal, *señor*; you are begging for your life.'

At that moment, both Prowler and Corsicana were resigned to this being the end. With no means of defence available to them, they stoically accepted the inevitable. There was a great dignity in the way they faced death.

Then the situation changed drastically and dramatically with a lightning speed that had Prowler, Corsicana, and the Mexican bandits momentarily bewildered. With a swishing, fluttering sound, an arrow came fast through the air. The pointed end entered the side of El Toro's neck, passing through to come out the other side and bury itself deep in the wooden side of the wagon, pinioning him.

Unmoving, Prowler, Corsicana, and the four mounted Mexicans watched in horror as the bandit chief dropped his rifle. Reaching up with his right hand, El Toro grasped the feathered shaft of the arrow that protruded from his neck. Pulling on it, he failed to extract the head of the arrow from the wagon, and the attempt caused him so much pain that he cried and snivelled like a baby.

Accustomed to being in charge of himself and all those around him, realization of his helplessness generated a rage in El Toro. He let out a mighty roar. Lurching sideways in an attempt at freeing himself, he tore his neck apart, ripping out flesh, veins, arteries, and his windpipe. Small bones coated with thick blood were among the soggy mess that came out of him as, free of the arrow that remained embedded in the side of the wagon, he slumped to the ground, his all but severed head flopping uselessly.

It was Corsicana who first snapped out of the torpid state brought about by the horrific death scene. Drawing his six-gun fast, he had shot one Mexican out of the saddle before the others came to life. One of them fired his rifle at Prowler, who rolled head over heels along the ground to where Corsicana had left the rifle. Unharmed, Prowler grabbed the rifle and blasted away, hitting the horse of the Mexican who had been firing at him. Mortally injured, the animal fell, and its rider was lucky to escape as it rolled sideways. But before the Mexican could regain his feet, Prowler had killed him with another shot from the rifle.

Ducking and weaving to avoid the bullets coming his way, Corsicana shot the third Mexican in the chest, sending him flying backwards off his horse. Panicking, the last remaining Mexican wheeled his horse about and galloped off.

'Have you ever shot a man in the back, Prowler?' Corsicana asked, casually, as they stood together watching the Mexican ride off.

'No, have you?'

'Not until now,' the young Mexican answered, reaching to take the rifle from Prowler and putting it to his shoulder.

Corsicana squeezed the trigger and the fleeing bandit threw both arms out and fell sideways from the saddle. Then Corsicana did a quarter turn, rifle held in readiness as he heard approaching hoofbeats.

'I guess that explains the arrow,' he said, lowering the rifle as Juanita rode over the hill.

'That's Dooley's horse she's leading,' Prowler said wonderingly.

With an indifferent shrug, Corsicana said, 'I guess that means we got one more to bury.'

Seven

They reached the deserted ranch at twilight, which made it all the more eerie. Every sound they made echoed hollowly. A milch cow raised its head to look at them in lazy curiosity, and chickens squawked and scratched about on cultivated ground. Everything about the place was right except for the total absence of human beings. Inside of the house everything was in order, with food and utensils in expected places, but there was no one to use either. It was as if whoever lived here had disappeared by magic.

Corsicana remarked jokingly, 'Nothing here but ghosts.'

'Apaches?' Prowler half-asked half-suggested, looking to Dooley for an answer.

'No,' Juanita replied firmly before Dooley could voice an opinion. 'If the Apaches were responsible we would find bodies lying around.'

Death Dances at Yuma

'But why?' Prowler asked, looking around him. 'This is a real good place, well looked after, so why would folk up and leave it?'

'No point in worrying yourself asking, Prowler,' Dooley advised. 'This country is full of questions that can't be answered.'

Juanita nodded agreement. 'That is so.'

Over the past week when she had nursed him back to health, Juanita and Dooley had become close. Dooley had returned to work only that morning, replacing a disgruntled Corsicana up on the wagon seat, with Juanita sitting beside him. The wound in his side was sore, but it didn't bother him, and the unhealed red, jagged scar on his forehead was no more than an ugly disfigurement that would fade in time.

'There has to be an explanation,' Prowler persisted.

'All I know,' Corsicana said, 'is that it was mighty cold out on the trail last night, and it will be real cold again tomorrow night. So I say that we light ourselves a fire and bed down so's we have one comfortable night.'

This idea appealed to them all. Dooley went outside to tend to the horses and mules while Prowler and Corsicana got a fire going in the huge grate of the ranch house, and killed chickens for Juanita to roast. They ate well, and built up the

Death Dances at Yuma

fire for the night. Dooley had brought in blankets from the wagons, and all four prepared their beds in various parts of the room. Prowler stretched out close to the fire, while Juanita chose a place by a wall that trapped the warmth, but avoided the sleep-inhibiting brightness of the dancing flames.

Caution made Dooley watch Corsicana covertly, who was bedding down in the deep shadows of a corner. Juanita had warned him: 'Watch Corsicana at all times, Josie. He has sworn to kill you.'

'Corsicana and me have an old score to settle, Juanita.'

'I gathered as much,' Juanita had said. 'What about you, Josie, are you as bent on revenge as Corsicana is?'

'I guess not, Juanita. But when he makes his move I won't back down.'

'You don't have to tell me that, Josie.'

Now, aware of Dooley's eyes on him, the Mexican spoke from the corner of the room with a soft chuckle. 'Don't lie awake worrying, Dooley. When I come for you it won't be from out of the dark, or from behind.'

'I'm not worried, Corsicana,' Dooley said.

As he settled down, Corsicana's final words were, 'You would be wise to start worrying, Dooley.'

Death Dances at Yuma

The night was quiet then apart from Prowler's low snoring. Dooley, though glad of the warmth in the room, slept lightly. This venture had cured his problem with alcohol. Now he had regained a future, and that future depended on the sale of the rifles loaded on the two wagons outside. He had expected Prowler to arrange for the wagons to be protected. To share guarding them and their valuable cargo with him and Corsicana. But this quiet area where someone had run a ranch in peace seemed to have convinced him that there was no need for such a precaution.

Knowing that there was nowhere along the Gila Trail that was safe, Dooley no more than dozed. It must have been past midnight when a slight sound of movement in Corsicana's corner of the room alerted him.

Lying absolutely still, Dooley could hear the Mexican make his furtive way to the door. Almost noiselessly, Corsicana opened the door and went out, closing the door softly behind him. Sitting up, Dooley buckled on his gunbelt then followed Corsicana out of the house soundlessly.

There was no moon, but as his eyes adjusted to the starlight Dooley could see the bulky black silhouettes of the two wagons. A horse made a spluttering sound with its mouth, and a low groan came from a mule as it moved clumsily. It was

Death Dances at Yuma

quiet then until the call of a night bird came from Dooley's left. There was an answering call from the right at the far side of the wagons. A third call came from the side of the house.

Becoming suspicious, Dooley tensed, ready for anything. But he wasn't expecting a figure to move in the deep shadows beside him, so close that they were almost touching. Dooley's right hand automatically went down to his holstered gun, but he didn't draw as he recognized the dark shape beside him as Corsicana. The Mexican signalled for Dooley to be silent, then held up a hand with three fingers showing. Corsicana pointed three times, each in the direction from which Dooley had heard the call of a bird.

He knew then that he had misjudged him. Rather than being up to no good, the Mexican must have heard something and had come out to investigate. A courageous man, Corsicana had been ready to face alone whatever danger the night held. There were Indians out there in the darkness, intent on stealing the two wagons. There were only three of them, which told Dooley that this was no raiding party, probably just three adventurous young bucks out to gain recognition within their tribe. However, he and Corsicana couldn't use their guns. The sound of gunfire in the night was likely to bring hordes of Indians down on them.

Tapping him lightly on the shoulder and making a gesture for him to stay put, Corsicana slipped silently away into the night. Sensing that the Mexican had gone round the side of the house, Dooley strained his ears and managed to hear the muffled sounds of a brief struggle.

Then Corsicana was back at his side and Dooley detected the unmistakable, dull smell of freshly spilled blood. The birdcall on the left was repeated, and the Indian near the wagons answered. There was silence then, and tension built up in the night air as the two Indians anxiously awaited a cry from their comrade beside the house.

Cupping both hands round his mouth, Corsicana called like a night bird. Then he and Dooley waited tensely to see if the cry would be accepted. There was some furtive movement out in the darkness. The Indians were satisfied that they were still three in number.

Signalling for Dooley to take care of the Indian on their left, Corsicana slithered off toward the wagons.

Moving stealthily through the brush in an arc, Dooley stepped very slowly as he neared where he estimated the Indian would be. Sooner than

Death Dances at Yuma

expected, he came up behind a young brave who was slithering away from him, snakelike on his belly toward the wagon. Dooley was about to pull his knife when he either made a detectable sound or the Indian sensed his presence. Whatever it was, the brave turned his head to look behind him, his eyes widening in fear as he saw Dooley.

With no time to draw his knife, Dooley leapt forward. Landing hard with both knees high on the young buck's back, Dooley grabbed his head. With one hand clasping the Indian under the chin and the other a gripping the back of his head, Dooley twisted the head violently.

In the silence of the night, the crack as the Indian's neck broke seemed as loud as a gunshot. The brave's moccasined feet drummed rapidly on the ground, and then he lay still. Getting off the dead Indian, Dooley made his way carefully toward the wagons.

As he neared in the dim light he could make out the figure of an Indian crouching against a tree. Guessing that the brave was awaiting the arrival of the Indian he had just killed, Dooley was puzzled by there being no sign of Corsicana. Then he saw the Mexican. Corsicana was up in the tree above the crouching Indian. Standing on a thick branch, he was ready to pounce.

Waiting for Corsicana to make his move, Dooley

Death Dances at Yuma

tensed in alarm as, with a loud crack, the branch on which the Mexican stood snapped. Plummeting to the ground, Corsicana fell heavily, and the branch of the tree came down to hit him hard on the head.

Even though he was stunned, Corsicana acted fast and instinctively to come up in a crouch to defend himself against the Indian. Quick though the Mexican was, the young buck was faster. Jumping on Corsicana, the Indian knocked him flat, face down. Straddling Corsicana, a knife in one hand, the Indian used the other to grasp the Mexican's hair and pull up his head.

About to slit Corsicana's throat, the Indian froze as Dooley came out of the night to stand close in front of him. Head strained back by the Indian, Corsicana's eyes met those of Dooley. There was no pleading, in the Mexican's gaze. Not expecting Dooley to save him, the tough Corsicana was resigned to his own death.

Dooley was in a dilemma. His sworn enemy, the man who intended to kill him, was about to die. The situation favoured Dooley. Cutting Corsicana's throat would occupy the Indian long enough for Dooley to kill him in turn. It was a simple solution, and Dooley hesitated. At that moment the doomed Corsicana smiled at Dooley, in genuine amusement at his indecision.

Death Dances at Yuma

That unexpected smile in the face of death goaded Dooley into speedy action. With the Indian's knife hand already on the move, Dooley lunged forward. A downward slash with his razor-sharp knife opened up the brave's arm from the shoulder to the wrist.

Sobbing in his agony, the young Indian fell off Corsicana, incongruously using his left hand in an attempt to push bloodied muscles, sinews and tendons back into the long, gaping wound that ran the length of his right arm. Coming up on to his knees, Corsicana ended the young brave's excruciating pain by plunging his knife deep into his chest.

Getting to his feet and without as much as a glance at Dooley, Corsicana turned away and set off in the direction of the house. Following him, Dooley saw that the Indian's cries of pain had brought Prowler and Juanita to the door of the house.

As soon as she spotted Dooley, Juanita started to run to him. An uncertain Dooley slowed his pace. He was uneasy about his growing relationship with the wild Juanita. Holly had been all he could wish for in a woman, and while Dolores Morello lacked the refinements of his late wife, she had a good heart and, though a saloonkeeper, she behaved decently. In contrast, he could vividly recall an uncaring Juanita as the Mexican bandit chief tore his own throat apart on the arrow she had shot through his neck. Whether or not she was of mixed blood, her savagery disturbed him.

Though he had intended otherwise, when she reached him now he allowed her to embrace him.

'The folk in the ranch house must have killed them,' Lieutenant Kearney said when Heuco showed him the last of three dead young Apaches.

Heuco shook his head. 'No, Lieutenant. These bucks were killed in the night, and no rancher would get into a knife fight with Apaches out here in the woods.'

Looking over to the ranch house, Kearney decided. 'Then I guess that we'd better ask the people in the house.'

'Nobody lives in the house now, sir,' the scout said.

'But. . . .' A bewildered lieutenant looked around him. 'This place is well cared for, Heuco. Look at the animals. They have been tended recently. Are you saying that Apaches killed the ranch folk?'

'No, there's no bodies,' Heuco answered. 'I'd say it was Mexican bandits frightened the people here into abandoning the place. Probably El Toro.'

Death Dances at Yuma

'El Toro, Heuco? Surely if he was in these parts we'd have seen something of him?'

'We have, Lieutenant,' the scout replied calmly. 'Those five graves we came across back along the trail where Prowler camped. I opened one of them up after you and your men had ridden out. El Toro was in it.' He pointed to several sections of ground in turn. 'Those tracks are made by wagon wheels, sir. The last to stay in that house was Prowler and his people.'

'How far ahead are they?' a relieved and excited Kearney asked.

'No more than a day and a half, Lieutenant,' the scout announced, before adding some advice. 'But we'll need to go in easy like. Prowler's got three others riding with him.'

The lieutenant was scornful. 'Three? I've got thirty men here under my command!'

'If those with Prowler can take care of these three Apache silently in the night, and kill El Toro and four of his gang, then you may find that thirty soldiers ain't enough, Lieutenant.'

'Hogwash!' Kearney said dismissively. 'Let's get mounted up, Heuco, and I'll move the troop out. Now that we're in spitting distance of Prowler I want to cover as much ground as possible in the shortest time.'

The scout delayed getting up into the saddle.

Death Dances at Yuma

He spoke quietly. 'One of them with Prowler is a woman, sir.'

'That doesn't alter anything, Heuco,' Kearney said, although he was taken aback by this news. 'If she, whoever she is, chooses to ride with a *mal hombre* such as Kane Prowler, then she must be prepared to face the consequences.'

'From the signs, Lieutenant, I'd say that she's either an Indian or a 'breed,' Heuco warned.

'What is your meaning?'

'Just that if you harm her you may find yourself facing not just Prowler, but the whole of the Apache nation.'

Thoughtful for a few moments, Lieutenant Kearney then raised himself up in the stirrups and signalled to his men. 'For'ard ho!'

The column of soldiers moved off with a determined-looking Matthew Kearney at its head. Riding at the lieutenant's side, the Indian scout leaned sideways in the saddle of his trotting horse to study the ground. They had covered only a short distance when Heuco kicked his heels into his mount and rode ahead watchfully.

In a thickening dusk, Prowler, Corsicana, and Dooley squatted, the hardness of their faces accentuated by the yellow glow of the camp-fire. They had picketed the horses and mules in a long

Death Dances at Yuma

line close to where the two wagons had drawn up. The camp was in the recess of a hill and the wily Corsicana had driven in the picket pins so that the horses were away from the only two approaches. If they should be attacked from one direction, then they could easily reach their mounts and escape.

'No Indian ever stayed in one place for long,' Prowler remarked, as he rolled a cigarette, pausing to lick the paper. 'I'll tell you both now, I'm uneasy about that girl taking off like that.'

'As you said, Prowler, you can't tie an Indian down,' Corsicana responded.

Dooley stayed out of the discussion. Juanita's sudden disappearance earlier that day had saddened him much more than it should have done, but he wasn't worried by it. He trusted her implicitly in the knowledge that she had already saved his life once. It occurred to him that she may have broken away so that she could watch over them from a distance. On the trail they knew little of what was going on outside of their immediate area, which meant that they could be riding headlong into danger.

He tensed as Corsicana made a sudden move in the growing darkness, but the Mexican was simply adding wood to the fire. Since they had killed the three Apaches, Corsicana had spoken to

Death Dances at Yuma

him just once, when they were harnessing the mules the following morning. Coming close to Dooley, and speaking quietly so that neither Juanita nor Prowler could hear, he had said, 'Nothing has changed, Dooley. I'll still come looking for you when we reach Yuma.'

Dooley had made no reply. Though he would carry Holly forever in his heart, she no longer spent so much time in his mind. Tres Piños and the joy and tragedy he had known there now seemed to be ages ago. It was so remote that it all could have taken place in some other world.

He was suddenly brought out of his deep thinking, becoming instantly alert, as were Prowler and Corsicana. Something had happened in the surrounding darkness, but none of them could identify what it was.

Then a movement, so faint that it could have been a harmless shadow animated by the scant illumination from a dying fire, had them reaching for their guns. All three relaxed as Juanita stepped silently into the light.

'Snakes alive, gal!' Kane Prowler protested. 'You're going to get your danged head blowed off, creeping up on folk thataway.'

Juanita said calmly, 'No, Prowler, it's you who'll end up dead if you don't know when there's someone moving in on your camp.'

Death Dances at Yuma

What she said was true. Dooley was ashamed to admit that it was a justified criticism of them all. Had Juanita been hostile to them, then all three of them would be dead now.

A grumpy Prowler was reaching for his blankets, ready to bed down for the night, when Juanita spoke sharply, stopping him. 'There's a column of thirty soldiers coming up behind us.'

'How close?'

Prowler's voice was hoarse and he looked anxiously at Dooley and Corsicana to see how they were reacting to what the girl had said.

'Close enough,' Juanita said evenly, 'for you to get those wagons moving on right now.'

Eight

Taking only short breaks of no more than two hours' duration, they had pressed on day and night. That way they had distanced themselves from the army column that Juanita had warned was trailing them. Now, with Fort Yuma less than a day's ride away, they could relax after weeks of continuous stress and strain. They had camped for the night close to the thriving cattle centre of San Escondido. After so long in the wilderness, seeing the blinking lights of the settlement in the near distance was alien and disconcerting. At first disorientated, they had returned to civilization, with great ranches and longhorn herds spread out through the surrounding valleys.

The hazardous trek was nearly over, and the prospect of financial reward for the hardship endured and perils faced was exciting. Prowler

Death Dances at Yuma

planned to set out at first light on horseback for Fort Yuma.

'I'll have made the deal with General Williams by noon, and be back here before sundown so's we can take the rifles on to the fort overnight,' Prowler explained, before pointing at Dooley to say, 'When the general passes over the money to me I'll pay you your share as we agreed back in Mesquite, Dooley. Corsicana helped out on this run when you were hurt, but he isn't my responsibility. Whatever is wrong between you don't amount to anything in this. It's up to you, Dooley, to see him right for money.'

As if he hadn't heard this, Corsicana walked away and pretended to unravel harness that was not tangled. Juanita shot a meaningful glance at Dooley. Whenever they had rested along the trail, Corsicana had ridden off and the sound of distant gunfire had reached them. Both Juanita and Dooley recognized that the Mexican was practising, keeping his gun hand in so as to be ready for Dooley when they reached Fort Yuma. He was obsessed by vengeance: focusing intensely on a shoot-out with Dooley. Prowler's suggestion that Dooley split his money with the Mexican hadn't interested Corsicana. He was certain that he would have the full share after gunning him down.

Corsicana was silent while they ate a meal that Prowler had prepared. As they were finishing their coffee, Prowler glanced around and raised his eyebrows in surprise. 'That dang girl has done lit out again.'

Until that moment, Dooley hadn't realized that Juanita had left. He had noticed her getting up from the fire and walking behind the wagons, but had expected her to return. In her usual style she must have led her horse away from the camp without mounting up. Where she had gone would forever remain a mystery. At no time had she ever offered an explanation on returning from one of her absences.

'Maybe she's gone to offer two wagonloads of rifles to her people,' Corsicana suggested cynically.

Aware that the Mexican was baiting him, Dooley stayed quiet. There had been ample opportunities along the trail for Juanita had she wanted to sell them out to the Apache. He had no doubts about her loyalty, and he was sure that deep down both Corsicana and Prowler implicitly trusted the girl.

'Where are you off?' Prowler enquired, as Corsicana heaved a saddle on to the back of a horse.

'I'm taking a ride into town,' the Mexican

answered, as he tightened the cinch under the horse's belly. 'I've forgotten what tequila tastes like.'

'I'm glad that I've forgotten.'

'You're not a Mexican, Prowler,' Corsicana pointed out.

Giving the Mexican a tight grin, Prowler retorted, 'That's something else I'm glad about.'

'Don't push too hard,' Corsicana hissed, as he swung up into the saddle.

Standing in front of the horse, Prowler stopped it by holding the bridle. He spoke in a voice that, though quiet, was laden with threat. 'Any time you want to try your luck, son, I'll be ready and waiting.'

Corsicana then leaned forward in the saddle to grasp Prowler's wrist and pull his hand from the bridle. Without saying a word, the young Mexican pulled the head of his horse round and jabbed lightly with his spurs. Riding slowly to where Dooley squatted by the fire, Corsicana reined up and sat in the saddle, a smile of derision on his face as he studied Dooley as if seeing him for the first time. Then he spurred his horse and rode out of the camp.

Coming over to the fire and hunkering opposite to Dooley, Prowler rolled a cigarette. Tossing the makings across to Dooley, he took a glowing stick

Death Dances at Yuma

from the fire to light up. Pulling smoke deep into his lungs, Prowler spoke contemplatively. 'We're at the end of the trail now, Dooley, and unlikely to need Corsicana's gun. I'd feel a whole lot easier if that Mex wasn't around.'

Lighting his own cigarette, Dooley sent a burning ember spinning back into the fire. Bright sparks flew in a dancing pattern in the darkness before they faded. Prowler wasn't exactly speaking of a double-cross. Corsicana was not a part of the gunrunning venture. They owed the Mexican nothing but a few days' wages, whereas Corsicana owed them for taking care of him when he was critically ill.

'Watch yourself, Prowler,' he cautioned. 'Trying to drygulch Corsicana could be dangerous.'

Giving an angry snort, Prowler snapped, 'I ain't never yet shot a man who wasn't facing me, Dooley.'

'Facing Corsicana would be even more dangerous than ambushing him,' Dooley predicted.

Sitting quietly, deep in thought, Prowler then spoke to himself rather than Dooley. 'I don't trust that Mex, and I don't want him coming back here tonight.'

Puzzled, Dooley wondered why Prowler had suddenly and vehemently turned against the Mexican. There seemed no reason for it. He had made it clear that any share due to Corsicana was down to Dooley. Fear didn't come into it. Corsicana was a seasoned gunfighter, but Prowler wasn't a man to be intimidated by that. If it came to gunplay, the Mexican, fast though he was, would probably be no match for Kane Prowler.

Seemingly reaching a decision, Prowler announced, 'I'm going into town, Dooley, and brace Corsicana. He's trouble, bad trouble, and if I don't do it now I'll have to take care of him at Yuma, and it will likely be too late then.'

When he had finished speaking, Prowler rose up and walked to his wagon. When he returned he was wearing a gunbelt. As he stooped to pick up his rifle, the slight bulge inside his jacket made by the derringer in the shoulder holster was noticeable.

Prowler was going after Corsicana, and that didn't sit right with Dooley. As Corsicana had said way back along the trail, there was unfinished business between him and Dooley. It would be wrong for someone else to get Corsicana. It would leave a void in Dooley's life that could never be filled, a debt to his late wife that could never be paid.

Getting up from where he had been squatting, Dooley stepped to block Prowler's way as he headed for a horse.

'Stand aside, son. We're partners and I've no fight with you.'

Death Dances at Yuma

'We are not partners, Prowler. All we mean to each other is the money to be collected in Yuma,' Dooley said tersely. 'If you want to go into town, then you've first got to get past me.'

Heavy face going white, Prowler looked undecided. 'You're good, son, and if we go on with this, one or both of us will finish up dead. That would mean that we came all the way down the Gila Trail for nothing.'

'So be it,' Dooley said with an indifferent shrug. 'The choice is yours. You can either back off or die right where you're standing. I'm too fast for you, Prowler.'

'What's your problem?' a perplexed Prowler asked.

'Corsicana's my problem not yours.'

'Are you telling me that you're about to ride into town?'

'That's right.'

Turning this over in his mind, Prowler then reached out to give Dooley a pat on the shoulder. He said, 'Good luck, son,' before turning and walking slowly back to his wagon.

'He's beaten us, Sergeant,' a disconsolate Lieutenant Kearney said as he lowered his fieldglasses.

Death Dances at Yuma

The column had slowly and tiredly negotiated Guadalupe Pass, close to where New Mexico, Arizona and Sonora met. Heuco had led them into a high-walled canyon and they had struggled under the handicap of fatigue to reach the summit on which Kearney, Larkin and the Indian scout now stood. Ahead of them the trail pitched down a thousand feet with a clear view stretching to a distant horizon.

'No sign of them, sir.' Sergeant Larkin commiserated rather than questioned his superior.

'How are you at producing miracles, Ken?'

'I don't think that is one of the duties expected of me, sir.'

'It should be, Sergeant,' Matthew Kearney said bleakly, as he stared at the empty miles ahead of them. 'Unless we can come up with a miracle of some kind, every white man, woman and child in this territory will be slaughtered when Prowler hands over those rifles to Chief Galvez Chama. What say you, Heuco? Are you a medicine man who can work magic for us reach Prowler before he gets to the Apaches?'

'I'm just a scout, Lieutenant.'

'And a damned good one at that. You were educated by the whites but have retained your native instincts and skills. At times like this I rely entirely on you,' Kearney complimented the

Indian. 'I would like to hear your thoughts on this, Heuco.'

'There's no way that we can catch up with those wagons now, Lieutenant. If Prowler has arranged a meet with Galvez Chama, then he'll turn off into the Chiricahua Mountains.'

'It would take a brave man to follow him into that territory,' a dispirited Kearney remarked.

'No, Lieutenant,' the Indian scout shook his head. 'Only a man who is pure loco would go into those mountains.'

'There's only one course of action left to us, sir,' Sergeant Larkin said gravely.

Kearney nodded in agreement, his rapport with Ken Larkin was such that the sergeant had no need to put his thoughts into words. 'I know, Sergeant. We have to get to the fort as quickly as we can and alert General Williams. How fast can we get there, Heuco?'

'Not quick enough, Lieutenant. The men might just about stand a final tough ride, but the horses would die on us. There's no way, Lieutenant, unless. . . .'

'Unless what, Heuco?'

Kearney was desperate for any suggestion. He was leading thirty men who were close to exhaustion, and the horses that Captain Blake had given them were now in as bad a state as the mounts they had replaced far back along the Gila Trail. He listened intently to what the Indian had to say.

Stretching a buckskin-clad arm, Heuco pointed north-west. 'Coker's ranch is an hour's ride that way, Lieutenant. It's a big spread and we could get fresh horses there. That's your quickest way to Fort Yuma.'

'Then that's the way we'll do it,' Kearney declared. 'Have the men move out, Sergeant Larkin.'

San Escondido was quieter than Josie Dooley had expected it to be. It was a town of dark shadows cast by the lamps of just a few lighted buildings spaced widely apart. Somewhere in the distance a dog barked continuously. Tying the reins of his horse to a hitching rail outside of a *cantina*, he looked for the horse Corsicana had ridden into town. But his own horse shared the rail with just two sleepy-looking burros with colourful blankets draped over their backs.

Easing his gun in its holster, satisfied with the smoothness of the movement, Dooley started toward the crude, curtained doorway in the adobe building. In a day or so he would be comparatively rich. With Dolores Morelos waiting for him back in Mesquite, the time had come for him to put the

Death Dances at Yuma

rest of his life in order. Top of the list was the very real threat posed by Alonzo Corsicana. Right at that moment the future reached only as far as a showdown with the vengeful Mexican.

Stepping into the dimly illuminated *cantina*, ready for action, Dooley was disappointed to find it occupied by only two people. A short, fat Mexican woman was in a corner of the room mixing something in a bowl. At the bar, a man in a huge sombrero turned his head to glance at Dooley, then looked away again.

Going back out, Dooley looked to where horses were hitched outside of an establishment further along the dusty street. It was too dark to see if Corsicana's horse was among them, so Dooley walked that way. Keeping to the shadows, he was watchful. He didn't expect Corsicana to shoot him in the back, but the Mexican was likely to gain the advantage with a surprise appearance. A shadow moved fleetingly in a gap between two buildings up ahead. Pulling in, his back tight against a wall, Dooley waited. But there was no further movement and he accepted that his imagination was playing tricks on him.

Continuing his slow walk to the second cantina, he tensed just a little as he recognized the horse that Corsicana had ridden out of the camp. Carefully approaching the door, Dooley kept most of his body concealed as he peered in. Cigar and cigarette smoke mixed with spiralling smoke from oil lamps to shroud the room in a dark grey cloud. Men drank at the bar, sat at crude tables, and moved about. It was impossible for Dooley to pick out Corsicana in the swirling indoor fog.

Resigned to having to go in to find his man, Dooley pushed himself away from the wall. Flexing the fingers of his right hand, he was moving toward the doorway when a voice coming from behind stopped him.

'I wasn't sure that you would come for me, Dooley.'

Swinging round, Dooley saw Corsicana, in semi-silhouette, standing in the centre of the street some twenty yards from him. Dooley stepped out to face him.

'I could leave it, Corsicana, but I know that you would push it. So here I am, and we can settle it now.'

'That suits me fine,' Corsicana said, as he took short, slow steps to close the gap gradually between Dooley and himself. 'It's Tres Piños all over again.'

This reference to the last time they had faced each other tilted Dooley's mental balance, as he guessed Corsicana had intended it to. He felt a drained, shaky sensation. Forcing the memory of

Death Dances at Yuma

that terrible day in Tres Piños from his mind, Dooley calmed down as he watched Corsicana's approach.

'Make your move whenever you're ready,' Dooley invited.

'It's your play, Dooley,' Corsicana retorted. 'I had the edge on you then, and I'm sure that I'm now even faster than you. It's your call.'

Corsicana had stopped walking now. He stood with his arms loosely at his side, but Dooley noticed the slight bend in the elbow, a hint of readiness if not tension, in the right arm of his adversary. There was an almost loud clanging sound to the seconds as they ticked by inside of Dooley's head. It had been a long time since he had faced a gunfighter in this way. His superb self-confidence of the old days had been eroded by doubt. Though his reflexes had been adequate during the emergencies that had occurred on the Gila Trail, it was inevitable that his long spell as an alcoholic had taken its toll.

'Damn you, Dooley, draw!' Corsicana hissed impatiently.

Gripped by an inertia that he feared was sponsored by a cowardice he had never before experienced, Dooley heard Corsicana curse and say that he would count to ten.

'One ... two ... three. ...' Dooley felt tension

building to an intolerable pitch, yet still he was held in a strange kind of paralysis. '... four ... five ... six ... seven ... eight ... nine...'

Suddenly, Dooley was aware of something kicking in. Maybe it was his self-preservation instinct, but whatever it was it freed him from immobility. Coming to life, he slapped leather. Immensely relieved to see that he had shaded Corsicana to the draw, he gave an involuntary cry of alarm, holding his fire as a figure leapt out of the shadows to stand between them.

Able to identify Juanita in the dim light, Dooley felt his knees threaten to give way and his brain start to spin. A long ago memory was resurrected and he found himself intensely reliving the scene in Tres Piños when his wife had died. The shock of it made him reel drunkenly, as he tried to make it to the side of the street, where he collapsed against the hitching rail.

A frightened horse moved, colliding with him, bringing him partially to his senses. He was vaguely aware of Juanita still standing defiantly in front of a white-faced Corsicana, who allowed his partly drawn six-gun to slide back into its holster.

Then he had the mind-picture again of Corsicana facing him and then Holly stepping out from nowhere, the impact of a bullet twisting her

Death Dances at Yuma

body violently. The unexpected appearance of Juanita had brought all the horror of it back. It was so vivid that Dooley blacked out.

He was aware of a supporting arm round his shoulders. Opening his eyes he was surprised to see that it was a concerned Corsicana who was holding him.

'How are you feeling?' the Mexican enquired.

'I'm all right now,' Dooley replied, straightening up and frowning at Corsicana. 'What's happening with you?'

'I guess we've both been loco, Dooley,' Corsicana answered sheepishly. 'We've spent years wanting to kill our own guilt, not each other.'

This made absolute sense to Dooley, but he hadn't expected to hear Corsicana saying it. He turned to scan the shadow-filled street. Noticing this, Corsicana informed him, 'She's gone. Juanita vanished as quickly as she arrived.'

That was typical of the mysterious Juanita, Dooley reasoned. She had intervened to prevent him from killing or being killed. Not knowing of the tragedy at Tres Piños, Juanita would be unaware of the waking nightmare her action had triggered in him. Corsicana also seemed badly shaken by it. Dooley had another question for the Mexican.

'What is this, Corsicana, a truce between us?'

Death Dances at Yuma

'I'd like it to be more than that, hopefully a peaceful understanding,' Corsicana said quietly. 'What just happened hit me hard, too, Dooley. It taught me that my brother probably deserved killing, and you were the law. And the truth of it is that neither of us will ever know whether it was me or you who shot your wife.'

Nodding agreement, Dooley said, 'Maybe from now on we both will find it easier to live with.'

'I sure hope so,' Corsicana sighed. 'Right now we could both use a drink. Come on, *compadre*.'

To his astonishment, Dooley found himself walking into the *cantina* with Corsicana as if they were a pair of old pals.

Nine

'At ease, Lieutenant,' General Williams, a tall, gaunt man given a doleful look by a sweeping grey moustache, ordered Matthew Kearney. 'This is a serious business, extremely serious, but it hasn't come about due to any failure on your part. This man Prowler had too much of a start on you when leaving Mesquite for you ever to overtake him.'

'Nevertheless, I led a failed mission.'

Kearney was contrite. They were in the general's office at Fort Yuma, a large room with austere, outsized furniture. The high-backed chair in which Williams sat dwarfed him physically, but in no way detracted from his forceful personality. Immaculately uniformed, the senior officer was every inch a soldier, and he had a presence that Kearney found to be intimidating. Williams was a man who would expect one hundred per cent from the officers and men under his command, but without asking anything of them that he wasn't capable of himself. The lieutenant felt that he had fallen far below Williams's standard.

Fixing Kearney with a steady but sympathetic gaze, Williams reassured him. 'I've had experience of the Gila Trail, Mr Kearney, and I would say that you deserve a commendation for getting to me so promptly with a warning of what had happened. It's thanks to you that I have the information that Galvez Chama has taken delivery of two wagonloads of rifles. Right now our priority is to limit the consequences.'

'Whatever action you decide to take, sir, I would like to be involved.'

'I will welcome having you with me, Mr Kearney,' Williams said, as a compliment to the lieutenant. 'What we need to do is to put ourselves between the Chiricahua Mountains and the ranchers. The hostiles must be contained.'

'With respect, sir, the Apaches will be fully armed and could well prove difficult to hold back,' Kearney observed.

'That is very true, Lieutenant. Though I would reject him in all other respects, I have the highest regard for Galvez Chama as a military commander. He is a brilliant tactician, Lieutenant, and

Death Dances at Yuma

consequently a formidable foe.'

'How do we stand with regard to numbers, sir?' Kearney asked.

'We don't, son,' Williams admitted. 'Galvez Chama's Apaches greatly outnumber us.'

'It seems we are to have quite a fight?'

'It's not so black as it may seem. We will take howitzers with us, Lieutenant,' Williams said, 'which will more than even the odds. Once out of the mountains the Apaches bunch up when they attack, and we can blast them to pieces.'

Standing up out of the chair that the general had earlier gestured him into, Kearney said, 'With your permission, sir, I will check that my sergeant has quartered the men.'

'Very well, Lieutenant Kearney. Make sure that they have a good night's sleep. We will set out at first light because the howitzers are a burden. I've known them to break down a set of mules in less than five miles.'

They moved off for Fort Yuma just before dusk. That way, Prowler had maintained, they would be skirting the edge of Apache territory under cover of darkness. He was on the lead wagon, while Corsicana rode on the second with Dooley, who found it difficult to have his former sworn enemy as a friend. But the atmosphere between them was easier than he had expected it to be. The aborted showdown seemed to have laid the ghosts that had been mercilessly haunting them both since Tres Piños. For Dooley it was as if Holly was at long last resting peacefully. His mourning no longer had its previous intensity, and he felt that his wife was urging him to get on with the rest of his life.

Prowler had been in his bedroll when they had returned late from San Escondido, so he hadn't questioned why Dooley had allowed the Mexican to return. Since then Prowler had made no comment on Corsicana's presence. To Dooley's disappointment there had been no sign of Juanita since she had risked her life stepping between them in town.

But now she rode out of the evening mist that turned the setting sun a dull orange. Reining her broomtail horse round, she rode beside Dooley's wagon. Looking straight ahead, she spoke in a monotone.

'Galvez Chama's warriors are dancing the death dance in the Chiricahua Mountains.'

Dooley uttered a low curse. Having suffered the hardships and perils of the Gila Trail, he now feared that the Apaches would attack before they could get the wagons to Fort Yuma. If that happened there would be no financial reward, no money as a stake for his fixture.

Death Dances at Yuma

'You'd better ride ahead and warn Kane Prowler, Juanita,' he advised.

'No,' the girl flatly refused.

Corsicana leaned forward on the wagon seat to look past Dooley at the girl. 'He has to be told, Juanita. They'll likely hit Prowler's wagon first.'

'Sure thing,' Dooley agreed, gaining comfort in a sudden idea as he voiced it. 'Maybe the army will send out a detachment to escort us to the fort.'

Turning her head to look steadily at him, Juanita said, 'There will be no soldiers, Josie. At Fort Yuma they know nothing about these wagons.'

'But...' Corsicana began an objection that petered out after the first word.

Not having for one moment suspected that Prowler's stated deal with General Williams was anything but genuine, Dooley was mystified by what Juanita had said. Prowler was both devious and unscrupulous, but Dooley couldn't think of any reason for him to lie about the consignment of rifles.

Dooley took up the protest where Corsicana had left off. 'But they must know, Juanita. Prowler went to Fort Yuma this morning.'

'Prowler is not to be trusted, Josie,' Juanita said insistently. 'I have been in the mountains, watching. This morning he did not go to the fort, instead he met with Chief Galvez Chama. Prowler will get a high price selling the rifles to the Apaches.'

Not having thought of this possibility, it perturbed Dooley to hear this. But the idea of Prowler having struck a deal with the Indians seemed increasingly unfeasible. He put his main point to Juanita.

'Why would the Apaches bother to pay Prowler for rifles they could ride in and take at any time?'

'That way,' Juanita answered, 'they would get only two wagonloads of rifles. If they pay Prowler he'll be back with more. If Galvez Chama is successful here, then other tribes will join him in an uprising. There will be a need for more rifles then.'

The logic behind this defeated any further argument Dooley had. Now frantically worried about the prospect of Prowler trading with the Apaches, Dooley said, 'Seems like you have it right, Juanita, which means that a whole lot of people are going to be killed.'

'That's so, Josie. The Apaches won't leave anyone alive.'

'Then we must stop it happening.'

Looking straight ahead once more, Juanita said, 'Only if you really want to, Josie. It is for you to decide. There will be no money to come from the

Death Dances at Yuma

fort, but the Apaches will pay up and Prowler will see you get your share because he'll want you on the Gila Trail with him again. If we manage to stop the sale to the Indians, then you won't see a red cent for all you've been through on the trail.'

'The money's not important; I don't matter,' Dooley said without hesitation. He had seen too many people, including innocent little children, slaughtered to let selfishness deter him from stopping the Apaches from going on the warpath.

'You have a good heart, *compadre*,' Corsicana acknowledged, with the hint of a friendly smile. 'I hadn't cleared leather last night when you had a bead on me. You would have killed me.'

'I'm sure glad that I didn't, *amigo*,' Dooley said. 'What about you? You helped out along the trail, so you should get what you deserve.'

With a harsh, short laugh, Corsicana said, 'With the kind of life I've lived, Josie, I probably deserve no more than a bullet in the brain. You and Juanita decide what has to be done, and I'll back you both all the way.'

'And you, Juanita?' Dooley enquired. 'You have earned your share in the rifle deal, so what do you want?'

'Nothing,' she answered, with a finality that forbade any further questioning.

Despite her good looks and ability to mix and

converse with people who had lived in towns, she was a primitive who didn't seek anything other than to enjoy nature, to roam free in the great outdoors.

Dooley changed the subject. 'How do you see us going about keeping the rifles from the Apaches, Juanita?'

'Prowler is pretending that we are heading for the fort,' Juanita replied, revealing that she had thought the whole matter through. 'But about three miles up ahead is a turning into the Chiricahua Mountains.'

'Pacheco Pass.' Dooley put a name to the turning to which he thought Juanita had referred.

'Yes, Pacheco Pass,' she confirmed. 'It will be dark by the time we get there. That is when we must make a move. Prowler will want to turn into the pass, but we have to stop him. We can't let him reach the Apaches in the mountains. Once the rifles are in Apache territory the whole US Army couldn't get them back. We have to overpower Prowler and take the wagons on into Fort Yuma.'

'That won't be easy,' Dooley said.

'Kane Prowler is one tough *hombre*,' Corsicana agreed.

Dismissing their reservations, Juanita said, 'He won't be expecting any trouble, so we'll take him by surprise.'

Death Dances at Yuma

'Whatever happens, Prowler will fight,' Dooley cautioned.

'Then Prowler will die,' Juanita said, unemotionally.

They swiftly put a plan together. It was a plan that had every prospect of success, and they began the first stage when the wagons were within half a mile of Pacheco Pass.

Juanita had dropped back to unhitch Dooley's saddled horse and lead it up. Turning the wagon over to Corsicana, Dooley moved over into the saddle. Reaching for the reins, he sent the horse at a trot to draw level with Prowler, who looked down at him suspiciously from the wagon seat.

'Have you got trouble, Dooley?'

'No problems,' Dooley reported. 'I just rode up to check that all was well with you.'

'I'm real glad that you did,' Prowler said, leaning toward Dooley to add confidentially, 'There's been a change of plan that I've been wanting to tell you about. Just by chance I have found myself an Apache chief who will pay four times more than General Williams for the rifles.'

'But the white settlers want the rifles to defend themselves,' Dooley complained. Putting his hands out each side of him, palms up in a so-what gesture, Prowler muttered, 'Business is business, Dooley. We'd be fools not to line our pockets, son.

By the time the Apaches put them rifles to good use, we'll be long gone, safely out of it. When the dust has settled, you and me will be back in Santa Fe planning another consignment of rifles. Not a word to the other two back there, but we'll be turning off a little way ahead for the Chiricahua Mountains.'

'I can't let you do that, Prowler,' Dooley said, catching hold of the rifle that lay across the stock of his saddle.

A barked order from Prowler froze him into immobility. Holding the reins of the mules in one hand, Prowler had his other hand inside of his coat. He said coldly, 'I've a forty-five aimed at your stinking heart, Dooley. One little move and you're dead.'

'I think not, Prowler.'

Juanita, who had silently ridden up at the other side of the wagon, stepped agilely on to the wagon seat behind Prowler. Moving with a grace that belied her violent intention, she used her left arm in a stranglehold round his neck. Juanita's right arm raised up high and was about to come down to plunge a knife into Prowler's chest.

Everything was going smoothly to plan. As terror widened Prowler's eyes, Dooley was bringing up his rifle when everything went suddenly and terribly wrong.

Death Dances at Yuma

With a blood-chilling howl, an Apache brave sprang out of the darkness on to the wagon seat to swipe Juanita hard across the head with the flat of a tomahawk, knocking her off balance. As she fell heavily to the ground, panicking the mules by crashing against them on her way down, she was in danger of being trampled. Dooley brought up his rifle with the intention of shooting her attacker.

But a second Apache appeared close to the head of Dooley's horse, yelling wildly. Eyes rolling in terror, the horse reared up. Fighting to control his mount, Dooley instinctively kicked his feet free of the stirrups to avoid being crushed if the horse should roll. Moving at an unbelievable speed, the Apache grabbed Dooley's right foot and heaved upwards.

Thrown out of the saddle, Dooley was half stunned when his head cracked against the side of the wagon. Before he hit the ground, hands were reaching to capture him, pinioning his arms to his sides. He heard Prowler shout, 'Don't kill him!'

Dooley was dragged to his feet and swiftly bound with ropes. He saw Corsicana, bloody, bruised and tied tightly with rope, dragged up to stand beside him. Prowler climbed down to stand looking at them, grinning. He shook the hand of

Death Dances at Yuma

an Apache chief, who pointed to where two bucks were at each side of a semi-conscious Juanita. They were pulling her along, her feet dragging, toes leaving grooves in the earth.

'These two are of use to me, Galrez Chama.' Prowler told the chief, pointing at Dooley and Corsicana.

Indicating the girl by inclining his head to one side, Galvez Chama asked, 'The woman?' Shrugging at first, Prowler then made a decision. He dragged the heel of his palm across his throat in a slashing motion. Accepting this with a nod, the Apache chief produced a wide-bladed knife and stepped close to Juanita.

Struggling helplessly against the ropes that bound him, Dooley shouted at Prowler, 'You can't let him do this, Prowler!'

Without looking round, Prowler swung his right arm behind him to slam Dooley in the mouth with a vicious backhander. Dooley sprang forward in a desperate attempt at crashing against the Apache chief, but a brave tripped him. Falling, Dooley's face smacked against a stone and he was bleeding from the re-opened old wound in his forehead as he was dragged back up to his feet.

Fearing the worst, he saw Galvez Chama twist his fingers into the hair of a barely conscious

Death Dances at Yuma

Juanita. Instead of slitting her throat as Dooley had dreaded he would, the Apache chief brought his face close to Juanita's and studied her. Apparently liking what he saw, he said something in his own language to the two bucks holding her, and she was led away.

There was a flurry of organized action then. Juanita was thrown roughly into a wagon on top of the boxed ammunition. Becoming animated as she regained consciousness, her wrists and ankles were tied. Prowler mounted a horse to ride with Galvez Chama ahead of the two wagons that were driven by Apache warriors. Nooses were placed over the heads of Dooley and Corsicana, and the other ends of the two ropes were tied to the rear of the second wagon. Needing to do a half-run to avoid being choked by the ropes around their necks, having difficulty with their balance because of their arms being lashed to their sides, they staggered along in great discomfort.

'Right now I wish you had gunned me down in San Escondido, Josie,' Corsicana gasped, as they jostled together while running.

'We'll get out of this somehow, Alonzo,' Dooley said, although he didn't believe it himself as they travelled further and further into the Chiricahua Mountains.

Death Dances at Yuma

'I'll settle for being free just long enough to kill Kane Prowler,' Corsicana said grimly.

With four howitzers placed strategically, General Williams had a curving defensive line stretching over half a mile south of the Chiricahua Mountains. The army guns and rifles had the foothills in range. Any emerging Apaches would immediately be cut down. Lieutenant Kearney's troop was mounted on fresh horses with orders to act as mopping up detail should any Indians be lucky enough to get round either end of the line. Messengers were riding to every ranch in the area with a warning.

'In my experience, Lieutenant Kearney,' General Williams began, 'the Apache, like the Mexican, has no taste for battle in the open. They'll soon realize that to venture out of the mountains is suicidal.'

Remembering the promise he had made to the glamorous saloonkeeper back in Mesquite, Kearney said with some trepidation, 'Apart from Prowler, I understand that there is one white man and a girl, possibly Indian or of half-blood, with the wagons, sir.'

'It will be a case of rough justice if Prowler should die in the battle to come, Lieutenant. As for the other man, I don't doubt that he merits a similar fate to that of Prowler.'

Death Dances at Yuma

Something of a romantic, Matthew Kearney had been unsuccessful in his attempts to get the image of Dolores Morelos out of his mind. Though it wasn't wise to tempt the wrath of General Williams, he felt that he owed it to the beautiful woman to make one more attempt.

'I believe that the white man with Prowler accepted the assignment in total innocence, sir.'

'Be that as it may, Lieutenant Kearney,' the general snapped tetchily, 'what would you have me do, risk everything in this fight for the sake of one man?'

'No, indeed not, sir. It's just that . . .' Kearney stammered.

'Do you see that howitzer over there, Lieutenant?'

'Of course, sir.'

'That gun is impartial and impersonal, young sir,' Williams exclaimed. 'Once fired it makes no distinction where its target is concerned. That gun knows of no reason to be selective, Lieutenant, and that is exactly how an officer of the military must be.'

'I do understand that, sir.'

Matthew Kearney explained and apologized inside of his head to the delectable Dolores Morelos.

Ten

The incessant chanting and the drumming of moccasined feet on the hard ground accentuated the pounding in Dooley's head. The fresh bleeding from the scar on his brow had crusted into a scab since the death dancers had begun their ritual some hours ago, but there was a throbbing ache behind his forehead that seemed to affect every nerve in his body. Together with Corsicana he was tied to a tree at the far end of the camp. The ropes were so tight that they restricted the circulation of blood to their limbs, and the rough bark of the tree trunk dug painfully into their backs.

Dooley couldn't understand why the Apaches had left them alive. Corsicana proved that he had been pondering the same question by remarking, 'They must have something special planned for us, Josie.'

Death Dances at Yuma

'It won't be an election to the tribal council,' Dooley prophesied with grim humour.

He had been watching the tepee into which Galvez Chama had dragged Juanita when they had been brought back to the Apache village. Nagged by worry over what was happening to the girl, Dooley's interest was sharpened as an obviously angry Galvez Chama came out of the tepee. An irate squaw followed the chief out of the tepee and the two of them stood arguing, voices raised and arms flailing.

Then Galvez Chama walked off on legs stiffened by temper. Within minutes, two bucks hurried into the tepee and came out with Juanita, each of them holding one of her arms. As they escorted Juanita away from the tepee, the squaw shouted abuse after her.

Brought to the end of the village, Juanita was tied to the same tree as Dooley and Corsicana. There was a large black bruise on her right temple where the tomahawk had struck her, but she was her usual confident self.

'I never thought I'd be grateful to a jealous wife,' she commented wryly when the two braves had left.

'Have you any idea what's going on, Juanita?' Dooley enquired.

'Prowler has given up on you, Corsicana,'

Juanita answered, 'but he's still trying to save you, Josie. He wants you to bring more rifles down the Gila Trail.'

'He must be loco if he thinks I'd work with him after he betrayed us.'

'I guess he figures that you'd do anything to get out of this, Josie,' Corsicana observed. Then he went on to give advice. 'If you are offered the chance to leave with Prowler, take it.'

'I don't think Prowler will get Galvez Chama to agree that I be set free,' Dooley said, 'and it would make no difference if he did. I'm staying with you two whatever happens.'

'Don't sacrifice yourself for us . . .' Juanita began, breaking off as a faint sound came out of the darkness.

All three of them tensed, listening. There was no further sound until a voice began whispering in the Apache language.

'It is Chief Orto,' Juanita told them. 'He says he is here for you, Josie. You saved his life, and now he will save you and us.'

'How?' Dooley asked, relieved but not yet building up his hopes. Orto could cut them loose, but they would never get away from the Apache village.

After listening to Orto's whispering again, Juanita reported back. 'Orto has only ten braves with him, so he cannot rescue us here and now. The army knows about the rifles and is waiting south of here for Galvez Chama to break out of the mountains. But Galvez Chama is taking his warriors out through Pacheco Pass to the east.

'*Madre de Dios*,' Corsicana groaned despairingly, at Galvez Chama's cunning plan. 'The Apaches will have slaughtered everyone in the territory before the army can move to stop them.'

'Hold it, it gets worse,' Juanita warned as she listened to Orto. She relayed more information to them. 'To fool the army and gain time, Galvez Chama is going to use us and some Pima Indian prisoners as a decoy. We will be taken south by a small escort of Apaches, and forced out into the foothills.'

'The army will kill us within minutes,' Dooley said miserably.

'No,' Juanita quickly explained. 'Orto says that he and his men will attack our escort before they can push us out into the open.'

'I hope that he gets his timing right,' Corsicana said laconically.

'Orto is leaving now, but he says that he will be watching over us at all times,' Juanita said.

Dooley spoke urgently. 'Before he goes, Juanita, tell him that we will need three horses at the foothills. We have to let the army know that

Galvez Chama has broken out through Pacheco Pass.'

Speaking rapidly in the Apache language, Juanita waited anxiously for Orto's answer before telling Dooley, 'Orto says that is difficult because he needs to move quietly behind the escort. But he has a boy with him who might be able to stay a little way back with horses for us.'

'Tell him that we must have horses,' Dooley insisted. 'If Galvez Chama spills the blood of white people all over this land, then the Great White Father in Washington will hunt down and kill every Apache, including Chief Orto and his people.'

'I will tell him, Josie,' Juanita said solemnly.

'The first hint of dawn, Lieutenant.'

General Williams pointed to the east with satisfaction. It had been a long, cold night, and the knowledge that the fight would begin at daybreak was heartening. Matthew Kearney had already checked with Sergeant Ken Larkin. His men were prepared to mount up and go in pursuit of any Apaches who might extend their breakout wide of the military line of defence.

Pressing a fist against his stomach, the general said, with a wry grin, 'No matter how many times a man goes into combat, Lieutenant, the old belly

Death Dances at Yuma

still knots up and there's a bit of a tremor in the hands.'

'Competition comes at a high price, sir, making us wonder whether we will win or lose, survive or die.'

'Nicely put, Lieutenant Kearney. I suppose those two worries, particularly the second one, is at the base of it all.' Williams nodded. He frowningly studied Kearney. 'You would seem a little preoccupied, Lieutenant.'

'It's nothing that will affect my ability to command my troopers, sir,' Kearney assured his superior officer. 'I am considering whether Galvez Chama will permit Prowler and those with him to live.'

'Most probably, Lieutenant. If he kills them he cuts off his supply of arms. Why the question? Surely the fate of a sidewinder such as Prowler doesn't concern you. Is it the Indian girl?'

'No, sir, I have never met her,' Kearney said, feeling foolish as he continued, 'It's the man who Prowler took on. I sort of made a promise to a woman back in Mesquite that I'd look out for him.'

'Something tells me that it is that woman and not the man who is on your mind, Matthew,' the general smiled.

'I guess so, sir. Are such feelings childish in a grown man?'

Death Dances at Yuma

'I have no idea, Lieutenant. I was twenty when I married Mrs Williams, and she has made sure since that I haven't had thoughts about other women. I take it that you will find a reason to stop off at Mesquite on the way back?'

'I intend to, sir,' Kearney said.

'Then I wish you ... hello! What's this?' General Williams raised his field glasses to his eyes. 'There's movement in the foothills. It is about to commence, Lieutenant Kearney!'

Chief Orto and his braves had silently and effectively disposed of the Apache escort that had brought Juanita, Corsicana, Dooley, and the Pima Indian prisoners to the southern edge of the Chiricahua Mountains. Three horses stood waiting in the brush. At a word from Orto the Pima Indians moved off to make their way back to their own territory.

'Chief Orto says he will stay with us to help fight Galvez Chama, Josie,' Juanita said.

'No, he can't,' Dooley said firmly. 'To the army an Apache is an Apache, and they will shoot him and his warriors down like dogs. Thank him for what he has done for us, and say that he must now go back to his own tribe.'

When Juanita had conveyed this message to Orto, the Apache chief made the peace sign to

Death Dances at Yuma

Dooley, who returned it before watching the courageous Apache and his braves slip away back into the mountains.

Looking out across flat land to where they knew the army was waiting, Corsicana asked, 'What do we do now, Josie?'

'I haven't figured that out yet, Alonzo, but whatever it is it has to be quick,' Dooley replied. 'Galvez Chama must be some way along Pacheco Pass by now.'

'One time I was with a circus as a trick rider,' Corsicana said.

Juanita looked bewildered by the Mexican's strange turn of conversation, while Dooley grinned. 'That's right interesting, Alonzo, but this is hardly the time for reminiscences.'

'That's where you're wrong, Josie,' a smiling Corsicana said. 'You see, I don't need reins to guide a horse, I can do it with my knees. If I ride toward those soldiers waving both arms, they will be able to see that I'm no hostile on the warpath.'

'Too risky,' Dooley decided.

'Do you have a better plan, *compadre*?'

'Not right now.'

'So, it has to be,' Corsicana said, as he walked to the brush and came back leading a horse. Making an Indian sign to Juanita, who reached out to touch his arm, he shook Dooley by the hand. 'If I don't make it, *amigo*, I reckon I'll find out which of us fired that fatal shot at Tres Piños.'

'That's not important now, Alonzo,' Dooley said feelingly.

Without another word, Corsicana mounted up and sent his horse at a gallop, reins dangling as he controlled the animal expertly with his knees. Riding a zigzagging course, the Mexican waved both arms wildly above his head. Neither Juanita nor Dooley took a breath as they watched the valiant Corsicana, both of them expecting that at any moment the military would open fire.

'Thank God!' Dooley exclaimed with a thankful sigh as a figure rose up in the middle distance, raising and lowering a rifle above his head. 'That's an army scout signalling for the troopers to hold their fire.'

Just as Dooley had finished speaking, a volley of gunfire shattered the morning air. Corsicana and his horse were caught in a withering fire that lifted them off the ground and cutting both the horse and its rider to pieces.

Corsicana was beyond help, but as the scout rose up once more to signal frantically, a deeply saddened Dooley told Juanita, 'It's all right, we can ride in now. They know not to fire again.'

'We are real grateful to you, and I apologize most

Death Dances at Yuma

sincerely for the tragic death of your friend,' General Williams said to Dooley, adding, 'You and the girl ride to the fort, mister.'

'No, sir.' Dooley objected, with a vehement shake of his head. 'Juanita and me will go after Galvez Chama. By the time you can get your soldiers up to Pacheco Pass it will be too late.'

'A lieutenant has already left with a mounted detail, Mr Dooley,' the General announced.

'How many men, sir?'

'Thirty.'

'Forgive me, General,' Dooley said, 'but your thirty men won't live for thirty seconds when they catch up with Galvez Chama's braves.'

Going to his horse, Dooley mounted up. Juanita, her bow slung on her back, was already in the saddle. They were reining their horses about when General Williams shouted at them.

'I forbid both you and the lady to leave this area, Mr Dooley.'

'We are not your soldiers, General, and do not have to obey your orders,' Dooley called back as he galloped away with Juanita at his side.

Not sparing the horses, they were soon close enough to Pacheco Pass to hear the sounds of battle. The screaming of wounded men and horses, and intermittent gunfire told both Juanita and Dooley that a hand-to-hand fight was raging just outside the pass. They reined in among trees, and Juanita pointed to the top of a steep cliff.

'There's Galvez Chama, watching the fight.'

Dooley saw the Apache chief sitting on a horse, flanked by a sub-chief on one side and Kane Prowler on the other, looking down upon the fray. Neither he nor Juanita needed to speak. They knew what had to be done. Wheeling their horses to the west, they rode to the foot of the hill that led up to where Galvez Chama was. Dismounting, they went up the hill together on foot, with Juanita fitting an arrow in her bow.

When they came up behind the unsuspecting trio, Juanita spoke one word gutturally in the Apache language. All three turned in the saddle. Juanita's arrow thudded into the chest of the sub-chief, the point coming out of his back strung with bloody tendrils of flesh. Recognizing Dooley, Prowler forced a grin:

'Josie, by God! Am I pleased that you're safe!'

The grin stayed engraved on Prowler's face as a bullet from Dooley's rifle carried away the top of his skull so that the contents of his head flopped out to splatter on the ground as he went sideways out of the saddle.

Keeping Galvez Chama covered, Dooley signalled for him to dismount. Juanita disarmed the chief, and Dooley used his rifle to urge him

Death Dances at Yuma

toward the edge of the cliff. It was all quiet down below now. There was a sheer drop to a scene of carnage. The ground was strewn with dead and dying soldiers. The victorious Apaches stood aimlessly looking up at the clifftop, awaiting orders from their chief.

Making a show for the Indians far below, Dooley first passed his rifle to Juanita, then unbuckled his gunbelt and handed it to her. She understood. Dooley wanted the Apache braves to see their chief defeated by him in unarmed combat. That would rob the chief of prestige, and leave them leaderless and too disorganized to go on the warpath. The ranchers would be saved. But both Juanita and Dooley knew that he was taking a big risk. Galvez Chama was powerfully built, and he now extended a heavily muscled arm that was as thick as the leg of an average man. Attempting to grab the wrist, Dooley discovered that the Apache chief could move with a bewildering speed that was astonishing in so large a man.

Grabbing Dooley's arm, Galvez Chama pulled him off balance, twisting Dooley round so that his back came against the Apache's barrel chest. Reaching down with his free hand, Galvez Chama gripped Dooley by a thigh. With a mighty surge of strength, the chief lifted Dooley high

Death Dances at Yuma

above his head, at the same time giving a roar of triumph that was echoed in concert by his warriors below.

Knowing that within seconds he would be thrown to his death, Dooley was desperate. Stretching down he jabbed two forgers hard into Galvez Chama's eyes. Agony galvanized the Apache chief into immediate action, but, temporarily blinded, he wanted to be certain where the edge of the cliff was before throwing Dooley. Galvez Chama's hesitation gave Dooley the chance to swing his body violently this way and that, rocking the chief off balance. Staggering backwards, Galvez Chama caught his heels against a stone and fell, dropping Dooley as he went down.

The Apache lay on his back as Dooley came up fast, ready to stomp on him with both feet. Rolling to one side to prevent this happening, Galvez Chama couldn't avoid two large stones. He lay face down on them, bridging one that was under his hips with another stone on which lay his upper chest.

Seizing the opportunity, Dooley leapt into the air. Bending both knees in the jump, he straightened his legs as he came down with both feet on the middle of the Apache's back. The Indian's spine snapped like a brittle branch.

Death Dances at Yuma

Dragging it close to the edge of the cliff Dooley bent to grip Chama's corpse by the long hair and breechclouts. Summoning up every vestige of strength in his body, Dooley raised the Apache chief above his head and locked his elbows, the strain of it obvious in his voice when he instructed the woman who was at his side.

'Tell them that Galvez Chama is dead, Juanita, and the soldiers are coming and they, too, will die if they don't go back into the mountains.'

Waiting until Juanita had shouted down to the Apache braves, Dooley then tossed their chief down to them. With Juanita he watched the body plummet down to kick up a cloud of dust as it hit the ground.

The Apache warriors walked slowly and silently to view what was left of the body. Then they collected their ponies, mounted up and rode back into Pacheco Pass.

Pleased to see the Indians depart, Dooley and Juanita ran down the hill to their horses and rode to the recent battlefield that was littered with the bodies of soldiers. Dismounting, they parted to walk among the casualties in search of any who might still be alive. Dooley found only one, a young lieutenant who held a shattered right arm as if trying to keep it attached to a shoulder torn bloodily apart.

Death Dances at Yuma

As Dooley knelt beside him, the lieutenant astonished him by asking, 'Are you Josie Dooley?'

Confirming with a nod that he was, Dooley queried, 'How do you know my name, Soldier?'

'There's a lady named Dolores waiting for you back in Mesquite, Dooley,' the lieutenant said, fighting weakness to force a smile.

Hearing a distant bugle, Dooley took comfort in the knowledge that the army would soon be here with a doctor. Liking the guts the lieutenant was showing, Dooley said, 'Maybe she's waiting for me, Soldier, but the way you spoke her name I figure I've got competition.'

'Not now you haven't,' the lieutenant rasped through clenched teeth. 'But when you see her, tell her that Matthew Kearney kept his promise.'

'General Williams will be here any minute now. You get the doc to fix you up and you can tell Dolores yourself.'

'Thanks for lying to me, Dooley.'

The lieutenant was suddenly convulsed by a spasm of extreme pain. The fingers that were clutching his upper arm straightened rigidly. The shattered arm fell away from his body, taking a portion of the chest with it as shredded flesh. A bugle sounded, real close now, but Lieutenant Kearney didn't hear it.

Juanita walked up to Dooley in her soft-footed

way. 'They are all dead over there, Josie.'

'It's the same here,' Dooley said, morosely.

Having slept badly, Dooley welcomed the first signs of dawn. Alonzo Corsicana and Lieutenant Matthew Kearney had haunted him throughout the night. He had camped with Juanita at Council Bluffs. Both of them were heading somewhere together, but neither of them knew where. They had talked when sitting at the fire the previous evening. A disgruntled Dooley had bemoaned the fact that he was as penniless now as when he had left Mesquite.

Elegant head tilted to one side as she listened to the creatures of the night, somehow communing with them, Juanita had said, 'Right this moment, Josie, at one with everything here in the wild, I am wealthier than the grandest of ladies living in a town.'

'I'm sorry, Juanita, but I can't see it that way,' he had apologized. 'I was supposed to make something of myself by going to Yuma. I was the town drunk when I left Mesquite, and I'll probably be the town drunk again when I get back.'

With a shake of her head, Juanita had said, 'She won't let that happen, Josie.'

'How did you know there is a *she*?' he had questioned, astounded by her powers of perception.

Death Dances at Yuma

'You are the kind of man who always has a woman close to him,' Juanita had replied. 'You are not a drunk any more, Josie, and regardless of money she will see you as a much richer man than when you left her.'

'If I shared your life I would have no need of money,' he had said, surprising both Juanita and himself with this concept.

Not looking at him, she had spoken softly, wistfully. 'We could be together, Josie. I would like that, but it is a big decision for you to make.'

'I'll decide in the morning,' he had told her gruffly, tormented by his emotions.

Having made that decision an hour ago, he now walked slowly and reluctantly to where she had bedded down under a tree. However she took it, telling her what he had decided was going to cause him anguish. But Juanita wasn't there. On the flattened grass where she had lain, three feathers from a wild goose had been placed. It was a message that Dooley understood. Juanita had known his decision before he had made it. She had left in the night, going out of his life as abruptly and mysteriously as she had come into it.

Not bothering with either a fire or breakfast, he rolled his blankets, saddled his horse and mounted up. For a brief moment he thought he

Death Dances at Yuma

saw Juanita coming out of the trees in her noiseless way. But it was an illusion. Pulling on the reins Josie Dooley brought the horse round and rode off in the direction of Mesquite.